새벽 출정

도서출판 아시아에서는 《바이링궐 에디션 한국 현대 소설》을 기획하여 한국의 우수한 문학을 주제별로 엄선해 국내외 독자들에게 소개합니다. 이 기획은 국내외 우수한 번역가들이 참여하여 원작의 품격을 최대한 살렸습니다. 문학을 통해 아시아의 정체성과 가치를 살피는 데 주력해 온 도서출판 아시아는 한국인의 삶을 넓고 깊게 이해하는 데 이 기획이 기여하기를 기대합니다.

Asia Publishers present some of the very best modern Korean literature to readers worldwide through its new Korean literature series 〈Bi-lingual Edition Modern Korean Literature〉. We are proud and happy to offer it in the most authoritative translation by renowned translators of Korean literature. We hope that this series helps to build solid bridges between citizens of the world and Koreans through rich in-depth understanding of Korea.

바이링궐 에디션 한국 현대 소설 020

Bi-lingual Edition Modern Korean Literature 020

Off to Battle at Dawn

방현석
새벽 출정

Bang Hyeon-seok

ASIA PUBLISHERS

Contents

새벽 출정

Off to Battle at Dawn

1

오늘 아침 윤희가 떠났다. 새벽 어둠이 걷히지 않은 농성장을 떠나는 그녀의 양손에는 짐가방이 하나씩 들려 있었다.

"졸업식 하고 나서 바로 돌아올게요."

몇 번째 똑같은 말을 되풀이하는 윤희의 얼굴은 어두웠다.

"그 전에라도 싸움 끝나면 곧장 달려와야 해. 우린 꼭 승리할 거야."

미정은 그녀의 등을 두드렸다.

1

Yun-hui left in the morning. She was carrying one bag in each hand as she left the occupied factory. The darkness of early dawn had not yet lifted.

"I'll be back right after I graduate."

She kept repeating the same words; her face was somber.

"If the fight ends before that, you'll have to come running back. We're going to win."

Mi-jeong patted her on the back.

One of the male unionists, on late-night guard-duty, emerged from the gatehouse. He glanced at

후반 규찰을 맡은 남자 조합원 하나가 수위실에서 나왔다. 가방을 들고선 윤희와 양쪽의 미정, 민영을 번갈아 쳐다보고는 질문을 열었다.

"나가는 거야?"

윤희는 대답 대신 고개를 떨구었다. 잘 가, 반쯤 손을 들어 보이고 나서 남자 조합원은 수위실 안으로 들어가버렸다.

윤희는 입술을 깨물며 공장을 둘러보았다.

"너, 세광 잊으면 안 된다."

민영이 윤희의 목도리를 여며주었다. 미정은 차마 발걸음을 옮겨놓지 못하는 윤희의 어깨를 꼭 껴안았다.

"아주 가는 거 아니잖아. 어서 가봐."

등을 떠밀려 돌아서 걷는 윤희의 발걸음은 무거웠다. 사거리의 가두 매점에 이르기까지 윤희는 몇 번이고 멈춰섰다. 그리고 한동안 뒤돌아보았다.

가두 매점 모퉁이로 윤희의 모습이 감춰질 때까지 미정과 민영은 정문 앞에서 지켜 서 있었다. 겨울 새벽 공기가 매섭다. 돌아서 걷는 운동장 여기저기로 안료 포대들이 바람에 쓸려다녔다.

"이제 몇 명 남은 거니."

Yun-hui as she stood there with her bags, then at Mi-jeong and Min-yeong, standing on each side of her, before he opened the iron gate.

"You're leaving?"

Yun-hui hung her head instead of replying.

"Good luck," he said, half raising a hand before he disappeared back inside the gatehouse.

Yun-hui bit her lip as she took a long look at the factory.

"You'd better not forget Segwang."

Min-yeong straightened Yun-hui's scarf. Seeing her unable to start walking, Mi-jeong gave Yun-hui's shoulders a squeeze.

"After all, you're not leaving for good. Off you go, now."

She gave her a push in the back. Yun-hui turned and started to walk away with heavy steps. Before she reached the kiosk at the crossroads, she stopped several times and looked back briefly.

Mi-jeong and Min-yeong remained standing at the front gate watching Yun-hui until she was out of sight round the corner with the kiosk. The early morning winter air was bitingly cold. As they walked back across the sports-ground, empty dye-sacks were being swept here and there across it by

미정은 혼잣소리처럼 물었다.

"71명요."

"많이 줄었구나."

미정의 허리춤으로 겨울바람이 휘감고 지나갔다. 민영의 긴 머리칼이 날렸다. 아직 동트지 않은 새벽하늘은 떠나간 윤희의 얼굴만큼이나 어두웠다.

같이 싸우던 동료가 농성장을 빠져나갈 때보다 맥 빠지고 가슴 쓰린 일은 없었다.

조합원들은 떠난 사람에 대한 얘기를 공개적으로 하는 걸 금기로 여겼다. 그러나 아침이면 밤사이 떠난 사람들이 누구인가 입과 입을 통하여 은밀하고 신속하게 전파되었고 그것은 조합원들을 예민하고 신경질적으로 만들었다. 위원장인 미정은 애써 대수롭지 않게 여기려 했고 상집간부들은 어차피 떠날 사람이었다고 자위했지만 누군가 빠져나간 다음날엔 농성장 분위기가 무겁게 가라앉았다. 갑자기 환자가 늘었고, 아프다는 핑계로 문을 잠그고 누운 조합원들은 총회에 참석조차 하지 않았다.

농성 100일을 넘긴 지난주부터는 한동안 뜸하던 떨어져나가는 사람들이 다시 꼬리를 물었다. 텅 빈 사물함엔 편지 한 장만이 남아 있기 마련이었다.

the wind.

"So now how many are left?"

Mi-jeong asked the question as if talking to herself.

"Seventy-one."

"That's down a lot..."

The winter wind circled Mi-jeong's waist as it passed. Min-yeong's long hair was blowing wildly. Still showing no sign of day, the winter sky looked as dark as the expression on Yun-hui's face.

Nothing was more disheartening and painful than having a comrade in struggle quit the occupied factory.

The unionists considered it taboo to talk openly about the people who had gone away. And yet, each morning, the names of thosc who had left the previous night spread secretly and swiftly from mouth to mouth, making the other unionists alert and edgy. As the head of the strike committee, Mi-jeong made an effort not to let their leaving bother her, and the union leaders comforted themselves by saying that they were people who had been bound to leave anyway, but the fact of the matter was that whenever someone left, the next morning the atmosphere always turned grim. Suddenly, there

'끝까지 함께하지 못해 미안합니다. 제가 없더라도 꼭 승리하기 바랍니다. 위원장님 죄송합니다.'

어젯밤에도 나가겠다는 뜻을 비춰온 조합원들이 셋이나 되었다. 미정이 놀란 것은 셋이나 한꺼번에 떠나겠다고 한 숫자 때문만은 아니었다. 그 셋 속에는 윤희와 순옥이가 끼여 있었기 때문이었다. 이 길고 힘든 싸움에서 가장 열심히 싸웠던 사람들 중의 하나인 윤희와 순옥이 떠나겠다고 나선 것이다.

윤희와 순옥은 서로 다른 산업체학교의 3학년과 2학년이었고 학생조합원들의 실질적인 지도부였다. 순옥은 사장집 항의 방문 때도 빠지지 않고 따라나섰다 중간고사를 망쳐 종아리를 시퍼렇게 맞고 돌아와서 민영을 울렸었다.

성북동에 있는 사장의 집은 성벽 같은 담벼락으로 둘러싸여 있었다. 늦게 돌아오게 될지 몰라 산업체 학생들은 빠지라고 했지만 윤희와 순옥은 한사코 따라나섰다. 까짓 놈의 학교 때려치지 뭐, 하고 호기까지 부리며 쫓아나섰던 순옥은 그날 있은 중간고사에 참석할 수 없었다.

사람 키의 두 배나 되는 담장 안은 들여다보이지도 않았고 초인종을 아무리 눌러도 쥐새끼 한 마리 얼굴을 내밀지 않았다. 원목을 켜서 만든 튼튼한 대문은 서른 명이

were more union members getting sick, and those claiming to be ill would lock themselves in and refuse to take part even in the general assemblies.

Since the previous week, when the occupation reached its 100-day mark, the number of people abandoning, which had dropped for a time, had picked up again. Empty lockers were left with nothing but a note reading, *I'm sorry I can't stick it out to the end. I hope you will be victorious even without me. Forgive me, Chief.*

Last night, three union members had indicated they were intending to leave. Mi-jeong was surprised, not only because there were three of them leaving all at once, but also because the group included Yun-hui and Sun-ok. These two had been among the most dedicated fighters in this long, difficult battle, yet they said they were leaving.

Yun-hui and Sun-ok, third- and second-year students from two different technical schools, were in effect the leaders of those union members who were students. Sun-ok had not even skipped the protest visit to the company president's residence, though it wrecked her midterm exams and she had come back with bruised calves, having been punished by her teacher, which had moved Mi-jeong to

달라붙어 밀어젖혀도 꿈쩍 않았다.

행여 그들과 눈길이라도 마주칠까 맞은편 담벼락 쪽으로 달라붙어 지나가는 잘 차려입은 사람들과, 그리고 가끔 지나는 광택을 잘 낸 고급 승용차들과의 거리만큼이나 순옥은 자신의 초라함을 사장집 대문 앞에 주질러앉아 확인해야 했다. 텔레비전에서 보았을 뿐 실제로 이렇게 큰 집들이 있는 동네를 처음 본 사람은 순옥만이 아니었다. 표적을 잃고 허탈하게 앉아 있는 조합원들에게 표적을 자처한 것은 경찰이었다.

"야, 공순이들이 왜 여기까지 와서 난리야."

"인천에 성냥 공장, 성냥 공장 아가씨야."

그래, 니들 잘 걸렸다. 상한 마음의 조합원들은 경찰의 방패에 한꺼번에 엉겨들었다.

"그래, 이 씨발 좆같은 새끼들아, 공순이다. 어쩔래."

"니들이 공순이한테 보태준 거 있어."

돌아온 것은 곤봉과 주먹 그리고 발길질뿐이었다. 그러나 물러서지 않고 맞섰다. 걷어차이면 넘어지고 짓밟으면 뒹굴며 싸웠다.

"죽여라 개새끼들아. 굶어죽으나 맞아죽으나 죽긴 마찬가지다."

tears.

The company president's house in the upscale neighborhood of Seongbuk-dong was surrounded by a high, fortress-like, stone wall. The students were told to stay behind, since they might only get back late at night, but Yun-hui and Sun-ok followed along doggedly. To hell with goddam school, Sun-ok had said defiantly, and as a result had missed that day's midterm exams.

They couldn't see beyond the walls that were twice their height, and not so much as a mouse put its nose out from inside, no matter how long they pressed the buzzer. Even with thirty people throwing their full weight against it, the stout wooden gate would not budge.

Sitting sprawled outside the front gate of the president's residence, Sun-ok was obliged to recognize how shabby she looked, in contrast to the well-dressed people walking along the opposite wall trying to avoid making eye contact with them, or the fancy, shiny cars occasionally driving past. Sun-ok was not the only one seeing a neighborhood with such big houses with her own eyes for the first time, instead of only on television. Deprived of their target, sitting there despondently, the union mem-

더 이상 맞서 싸울 기력마저 상실했을 때 조합원들은 설움이 복받쳤다. 길거리에 아무렇게나 드러누운 채 서로의 멍든 얼굴과 찢긴 옷가지를 바라보며 소리내어 울었다.

"언니, 우리 사장새끼 죽여버리고 끝내자."

순옥의 저주가 미정의 가슴을 후벼팠다.

"그래, 김세호 사장 꼭 무릎 꿇리자. 우리 앞에."

경찰은 부둥켜안고 떨어지지 않으려는 조합원들을 하나씩 떼어내어 거지 내몰듯 동네 아래로 밀어붙였다. 그러고는 서너 명씩 한꺼번에 달려들어 사지를 들고 닭장차에 실었다. 그날밤을 조합원들은 생전 처음 가본 경찰서 보호실 철창 안에서 보내야 했다.

순옥은 학교에서 중간고사가 치러지고 있을 시간에 경찰서 철창 속에서 노동해방가를 부르고 있었다. 스물아홉 살이나 되는 미정도 웬지 주눅이 드는 경찰서에서 끝까지 진술서 작성을 거부하던 순옥이었다.

태평하다 못해 철없어 보이기까지 한 윤희의 경찰서에서의 행동은 긴 세광 투쟁 과정에서 잊혀지지 않는 일화 중의 하나로 남아 있다.

너도, 너도, 너도, 너도 말 안 할 거야. 모두들 입을 굳

bers soon became the target of the police.

"Why have you factory girls come making trouble up here?" the police shouted.

"Women from the match factory, the Incheon match factory!" the police sang.

Right, now you're really going to get it! The offended unionists pressed together against the policemen's shields.

"Fucking pricks! So we're factory girls—what about it?"

"What have you ever done for us factory girls?"

What came in return were clubs, fists, and kicks. But the unionists stood their ground and didn't retreat. They fell to the ground when they were kicked, rolled over when they were trampled, and went on fighting.

"Kill us all, you assholes. It's all the same for us whether we starve or get the life beaten out of us."

They fought back until they had no more fight left in them and sorrow came welling up. They lay on the street weeping and taking in each other's bruised faces and torn clothing.

"Sis! Let's kill that bastard of a boss and be done with it!"

Sun-ok's curse pierced Mi-jeong's heart.

게 봉하고 이름조차 대지 않고 있는 가운데 조사 경찰의 지적이 윤희에게까지 갔을 때였다.

"너 이름 뭐야?"

"깡순이."

윤희가 퉁명스럽게 내뱉었다. 세광 조합원들은 자신들을 깡다구로 뭉친 세광 깡순이라고 불렀다.

"강순희."

조사 경찰은 아주 흐뭇한 표정이 되어 보고서에 이름을 기록했다.

"생년월일은?"

"깡순이."

"이름은 강순희고, 생년월일 말야, 생년월일."

"깡순이."

"강순희, 네 이름 말고 생년월일을 대란 말야."

"깡순이."

조합원들이 더 참지 못하고 와 폭소를 떠뜨렸다. 뒤늦게야 자신의 아둔함을 깨달은 조사 경찰은 얼굴이 시뻘겋게 달아올랐다. 무안을 당한 조사 경찰은 윤희의 뺨을 세차게 후려쳤고 그 손자국은 며칠간 지워지지 않았다.

그렇게 당하고 와서도 남은 조합원들에게 세광 깡순이

"You got it! We'll bring Mr. Kim Se-ho to his knees. Right in front of us!"

As the unionists clung together to avoid being felled, the police tore them apart one by one and forced them down out of the neighborhood as if they were expelling beggars. Then the police, in groups of three and four, started rounding up the unionists, grabbing them by their arms and legs then throwing them into the police van with its chicken-wire windows. For the first time in their lives, the unionists were obliged to spend the night behind bars in a police station detention cell.

At the time the midterm exam was being given at school, Sun-ok was behind bars in a police station singing the Workers' Liberation song. Even Mi-jeong, who was twenty nine, was intimidated by the police station, but Sun-ok absolutely refused to write any kind of statement.

Although she seemed so very quiet, even childlike, Yun-hui's behavior at the police station remained as one of the most memorable anecdotes of the lengthy Segwang labor dispute.

"You, and you, and you, and you too, you won't say a word?"

All of them, mouths shut tight, refused to give so

답게 당당히 싸우고 왔다고 보고하는 윤희와 순옥을 보며 미정은 속으로 울었다. 조합원들은 말하지 않아도 멍든 얼굴과 옷핀으로 여민 옷자락과 하나같이 잠겨버린 목소리에서 그들이 어떻게 싸우고 돌아왔는지 알 수 있었다. 순옥은 신발마저 잃어버린 맨발로 있었다. 윤희는 그날부터 동료들에게서 강순희로 불렸다.

어느 조합원 하나 소중하지 않은 사람은 없었지만 윤희와 순옥만은 떠나보내고 싶지 않았다.

"등록금, 이틀 안에 마련될 거야."

"난 중학교밖에 다니지 않아서 잘 모르지만 며칠 늦는다고 퇴학이야 시키겠니."

미정과 민영은 참아보자는 말밖에 할 수가 없었다. 시선을 발끝에 고정시킨 윤희는 말이 없었다. 손매듭만 매만지며 순옥은, 미안해요란 말만 되풀이했다.

"자, 그럼 얘기 끝난 거다. 니들 등록금은 이틀 안에 틀림없이 위원장인 내가 마련한다. 그리고 나간다는 얘기는 없었던 거야."

미정이 필요 이상의 큰소리로 못을 박았다.

"돈 때문이 아녜요."

윤희가 먼저 입을 열었다.

much as their names, and finally the policeman charged with the investigation pointed at Yun-hui.

"What's your name?"

"Kkangsuni."

She spat it out rudely. That was what the Segwang union members called themselves, using a slang name meaning tough, gutsy girls.

"Kang Sun-hui."

The policeman repeated it, looking satisfied, and wrote the name down on the report form.

"Date of birth?"

"Kkangsuni."

"I got your name, Kang Sun-hui. I need your date of birth."

"Kkangsuni."

"Kang Sun-hui, not your name. Tell me your date of birth!"

"Kkangsuni."

The unionists could no longer control themselves, and they all burst into peals of laughter. Belatedly, the policeman realized he was being made a fool of, and he turned beet-red. Humiliated, the policeman slapped Yun-hui roughly across the face. The mark of his hand did not fade for several days.

Mi-jeong wept inwardly as she watched the two

"아니면, 얘길 해야 알 거 아냐. 집에 무슨 일이 있어?"

순옥이 대답 대신 종이 한 장을 내밀었다.

"등록금 좀 부쳐달라고 시골에 편지했더니 돈은 오지 않고 이것만 왔어요."

부모님전. 댁내 두루 평안하심을 앙망하나이다. 일전에 보내드린 서신에서 밝힌 바와 같이 회사는 일 년간 두 번 있은 노사분규로 인한 주문 단절, 경영 악화 등 여러 면에서 어려운 국면에 처하여 어쩔 수 없이 폐업을 결행하였습니다. 10여 년간 피땀 흘려 내 자식보다도 더 소중하게 일궈놓은 공장의 폐업을 결행하였을 때는 큰 고통이 있었으며 어떻게 하든지 가동하여보려고 하였지만 역부족이었습니다. 회사는 퇴직금 및 기타 수당 등 임금을 정산하고 있는 바 300여 명 중 220여 명의 사원들이 임금 정산을 받고 다른 직장을 찾아서 취업을 하고 있으나 댁의 자녀를 비롯한 80여 명의 사원이 임금 정산을 거부한 채 날이 점점 추워짐에도 대책없이 노동부 및 학교에서의 다른 직장 취업 알선도 거부한 채 차가운 기숙사 방에 기거하면서 일부 운동권 학생 및 위장 취업자들의 압력과 달콤한 말에 현혹되어 위장 폐업 철회하라는 억지를 부리며 점거

girls, Yun-hui and Sun-ok, report to the other unionists about how bravely they had fought—like two real Segwang *kkangsuni*—despite all they had been through. Even if they hadn't said a word, their bruised faces, their tattered clothes held together with safety pins, and their hoarse voices told the story of their battle. Sun-ok was barefoot, having lost her shoes in the scuffle. And Yun-hui became known as Kang Sun-hui from that day on.

There was not a single union member whom Mi-jeong did not value dearly, but she hated to see Yun-hui and Sun-ok, in particular, go.

"It'll only take a couple of days to get the tuition together."

"Look, I never got past middle school, so I don't really know, but surely they don't kick you out of school if your tuition is a few days late?"

Mi-jeong and Min-yeong could do nothing more than offer words of encouragement. Yun-hui kept her eyes glued to the tips of her toes and said nothing. Sun-ok kept rubbing her finger joints and apologized again and again.

"Let's just finish this conversation, shall we? I'm the committee chairwoman, and I'm going to make sure your tuition is ready in two days. Let's pretend you

농성을 계속하고 있습니다. 기숙사에서 나오고 싶어도 나오지 못하는 농성사원 중에는 부모님께서 상경하여 "내 딸 내가 데려가겠다"고 호통을 하여, 다른 농성사원에게 영향이 미칠까 봐 두려워한 주동자들이 기숙사에서 내보내준 예도 여러 번이나 있습니다. 학생들 중에는 등록금 및 제비용을 납부치 못하여 학업 중단까지도 초래될 입장에 놓여 어떠한 비행을 저지를지 모를 상황입니다. 귀댁 자녀의 장래를 생각하여 부디 상경하시어 임금 정산도 받으시고 농성장에 갇힌 자녀를 꼭 구해가시기를 부탁드립니다.

세광물산주식회사 사장 김세호 드림 (02) 752-××37

공문을 읽어내려가는 미정의 손끝이 파르르 떨렸다.

"이건 학교에서 보낸 거예요."

윤희도 종이 한 장을 내밀었다.

학부모님께. 본교에 재학중인 귀댁의 자녀가 취업하고 있는 회사에서 불법 집단행동에 가담하여 사회적으로 커다란 물의를 일으키고 있습니다. 막중한 교육의 책임을 맡고 있는 우리 학교 당국에서는 수차에 걸쳐 불법 집단

never said you'd leave," Mi-jeong said rather loudly in an intentionally exaggerated voice.

"It's not because of the money."

Yun-hui was the first to speak.

"Well, what is it then? How am I supposed to know if you don't tell me? Is something wrong at home?"

Instead of replying, Sun-ok held out a sheet of paper.

"I asked my parents for help with the tuition, but this came instead."

Dear Parents,

I hope this finds you well.

As I explained in a previous letter, the two labor disputes that have taken place in the last year have caused a loss of orders and a deterioration in operating conditions so that under these difficult circumstances, the company has found itself obliged to close down. This decision to close the factory has been an extremely painful one, as I have sweated blood to build up the factory over the last ten years, regarding it as more precious than my own family. I have tried my utmost to keep it going, but it was beyond my power. The company having calculated

행동을 중단토록 촉구하였으나 유독 귀댁의 자녀만 이를 거부하고 있는 실정입니다. 학교로서도 더이상의 선도가 불가능하다는 우려를 하지 않을 수 없게 되어 마지막으로 학부모님께서 직접 선도토록 당부키로 하였습니다. 만약 귀댁의 자녀가 계속하여 불법 집단행동에 가담할 경우 학교 당국으로서는 제적조치를 취하지 않을 수 없음을 거듭 알려드립니다.

한신실업고등학교장

"당장 나오지 않으면 아빠가 올라오시겠대요."

순옥은 민영의 어깨에 얼굴을 묻었다. 민영은 아무 말도 할 수 없었다.

"아빠가 무서워서가 아녜요. 이젠 정말 싸우는 게 자신이 없어요. 사람들이 무서워요. 싫고. 난 여기 나가도 다시는 학교를 다니지 않을 거예요."

"김세호 이 씨팔새끼. 우리가 언제 누굴 가둬뒀다는 거야. 개자식, 거짓말은 왜 해."

미정의 거친 숨결이 옆에까지 들렸다. 공문을 움켜쥔 손등의 혈관이 파랗게 내비쳤다.

"선생이란 것들까지 이럴 수가 있어. 학교가 도대체 뭐

a wage settlement composed of severance pay combined with other benefits, 220 out of the 300 employees have accepted the offer and are in the process of being rehired in other places of employment. However, your child is among those 80 who have refused to accept the offer and while the weather is growing colder, they are refusing the help offered by the Ministry of Labor and their schools in finding employment elsewhere, and instead are living in cold dormitory rooms. They have been duped by the pressure and sweet words of students and student activists who have infiltrated the factories, stubbornly demanding a reversal of the company shutdown, and continuing to occupy the factory. There have even been several incidents when the parents of some of the strikers, who wished to leave the dormitory but were not able to, have come up to Seoul and shouted 'I'm going to take my daughter with me,' at which the leaders have allowed them out of the dormitory, fearing that they might have an adverse effect on the other strikers.

There is no telling what misdeeds may result from the failure by those who are students to pay school fees or other expenses and risk being expelled from

야. 교육이란 게 뭐야."

"다 똑같은 인간 백정 같은 새끼들이야."

농성에 참여한 산업체 야간학생들은 매일같이 교무실에 불려다녔다. 농성이탈과 노조탈퇴를 종용받지 않은 조합원은 없었다.

수업시간에도 세광 조합원들만 지적당했고 수모를 겪었다.

"하라는 공부나 잘해. 그렇게 해서 언제 공순이 신세를 면할래."

견디지 못한 조합원들의 일부는 학교를 포기했다. 그보다 많은 숫자의 조합원들이 학교를 선택하고 농성장을 떠났다.

"위원장님은 사람들이 빠져나가는 게 두려워요?"

"아니, 안타까운 거지. 조금만 더 밀어붙이면 되는데……"

"순옥이 문제는 어떻게 할 거예요?"

"노조에서 부모님들께 일단 편지를 보내야지."

어젯밤 끝까지 대답을 않던 순옥은 떠나지 않았다. 혼자 있고 싶다는 걸 민영이 억지로 데리고 잤다. 새벽녘에 민영이 깨어났을 때 옆자리가 비어 있었다. 깜짝 놀라 자

school. Please consider your child's future, come up to Seoul, accept the offered wage package, and rescue your child held captive in the occupied factory.

Sincerely yours,

President Kim Se-ho

Segwang Manufacturing, Inc.

Tel. (02) 752-XX37

Mi-jeong's hands trembled as she read the letter.

"And this came from my school," Yun-hui said, holding out another sheet of paper.

Dear Parents,

This is to inform you that your daughter, currently enrolled as a student in our school, is employed in a company where she is taking part in illegal activities that are causing great social disturbance. As the authority responsible for the education of your daughter, we have, on several occasions, urged her to discontinue her involvement in these illegal activities, but she has consistently resisted our appeals. As we feel we no longer have any options, we turn to you, her parents, as a last resort in this matter. We would like to emphasize that, should your daughter go on participating in these illegal activi-

리에서 일어났는데 순옥은 한쪽 구석에 쪼그리고 앉아 편지를 적고 있었다.

"누구에게 쓰는 거니?"

"집."

"떠나지 않을 거니?"

순옥은 천천히 고개를 끄덕였다.

"민영이 네가 순옥이 좀 잘 보살펴줘라."

"위원장님, 지금 순옥이 걱정할 게 아니라 제 걱정부터 하셔야 할 거예요. 나도 언제 짐 챙길지 몰라요."

미정이 민영에게 발길질 시늉을 했다.

"그래, 나 죽는 것 보려면 무슨 짓 못 하겠냐."

"농담 아녜요."

"그래 임마. 나도 농담 아냐."

미정은 쓴웃음을 던지고는 목소리를 높여 말을 바꾸었다.

"오늘 아침은 뭐냐."

"감자국요."

"맛있게 끓여라. 식사당번은 내가 깨워서 내려보낼게."

민영은 미정과 갈라져 식당으로 향했다.

ties, then the school authorities would have no other choice but to expel her.

Signed,
Principal
Hansin Industrial High School

"My father says he's coming up immediately if I don't quit."

Sun-ok buried her face in Min-yeong's shoulder. Min-yeong was speechless.

"It's not that I'm scared of him. I just don't have it in me to fight anymore. I'm scared of people. I hate them. I'm not going back to school when I quit here, either."

"That bastard Kim Se-ho! Since when do we lock people up? Why docs he tell such goddam lies?"

Mi-jeong's rough breathing could be heard clearly. The veins in the backs of her hands shone blue as she clutched the letters.

"And your so-called teachers—how dare they? What the hell is school for? What is education for?"

"Butchers, they are, every goddam one of them."

Those strikers who were attending night classes got called to the teachers' room every evening. All without exception were advised to disassociate

어디가 고장인지 다단식 증기 취사기는 끝내 꿈쩍도 않았다. 식사는 식빵으로 대신할 수밖에 없었다. 민영이 공단 주변을 모조리 뒤져 식빵을 구해 왔을 때까지 상례와 금주는 취사기 주변을 맴돌고 있었다.

12월에 접어들고 찬바람이 불어닥쳤다. 107일째 접어드는 농성장에도 어려움이 몰려왔다. 날마다 곤두박질쳐온 날씨는 오늘 아침 수은주를 영하 10도로 끌어내렸다. 며칠째 계속되는 영하의 날씨를 조합원들은 제 체온 하나로 버텨야 했다. 감기에 걸리지 않은 사람이 드물었다. 4/4분기 등록금을 내지 못한 학생조합원들은 이틀째 등교를 포기하고 있었다. 윤희가 떠난 오늘 아침에는 취사기마저 고장이 나버렸다.

민영은 식당에 들어서는 조합원들을 바로 쳐다볼 수 없었다. 언니, 오늘은 메뉴가 뭐야, 언제나처럼 약간은 미안스러운 표정으로 식당에 들어서던 조합원들은 배식구 앞에 놓인 식빵을 보고는 이내 표정이 굳었다. 밤새 추위에 떨다 따뜻한 국물이라도 먹을까 생각하며 내려왔을 그들이었다.

식빵 네 조각씩을 받아든 조합원들의 표정은 날씨보다 더욱 스산했다. 민영의 눈치를 살피며 한두 입 베어문 뒤

themselves from the strike and quit the labor union.

During the classes, too, the Segwang union members were singled out and humiliated.

"Just study what you're told to study. Then you'll be able to avoid ending up as a mere factory girl."

Some of the unionists quit school because they couldn't stand it. But most of them chose to stay in school and abandon the sit-in.

"Chief, does it scare you that people are dropping out?"

"No, it's just a shame. If they'd only held out a bit longer..."

"What are you going to do about Sun-ok?"

"The labor union has to write her parents a letter."

Though she had refused to give a clear answer the previous evening, Sun-ok did not leave. She said she wanted to be alone, but Min-yeong took her to sleep beside her. When Min-yeong woke at dawn, the space next to her was empty. Startled, she jumped to her feet only to find Sun-ok hunched in a corner, writing a letter.

"Whom are you writing to?"

"My parents."

"You're not leaving, then?"

Sun-ok nodded slowly.

식당을 나갔다. 아예 입에 대지도 않고 짬밥통에 내던지는 조합원도 있었다.

"이걸 처먹으라고 내놓은 거야?"

경자는 받아든 식빵을 고스란히 짬밥통에 던져넣었다. 시위였다.

장기농성으로 지칠 대로 지친 조합원들의 감정은 송곳처럼 날카로웠다. 이 싸움 과정에서 그들을 따뜻하게 받아주는 곳은 어느 곳에도 없었다.

적개심. 가는 곳마다 자리잡은 가진 자들의 튼튼한 장벽 앞에서 조합원들의 가슴속에는 분노를 넘어선 적대감이 고스란히 쌓여갔다. 본사는 물론 노동청과 노동부, 정당, 그 어느 곳 하나 사장의 편이 장벽을 치고 있지 않은 곳은 없었다. 그리고 경찰은 그때마다 빠지지 않았다. 감당하기 어려운 분노와 적개심은 때로 동료들을 그 표적으로 삼기까지 했다. 힘겨운 싸움 속에서 여유와 너그러움을 잃어가는 조합원들의 가슴속은 동료 하나를 받아들일 공간조차 남아 있지 않았다. 승리에 대한 확신이 흐려져 감에 따라 강화되어오던 단결력도 질시와 반목으로 변해갔다.

"야이 썅년아. 처먹기 싫음 말지, 왜 처버리니?"

"Min-yeong, you need to take good care of Sun-ok."

"Chief, this is no time to worry about Sun-ok. You should be worrying about me. You never know when I'll be packing my bags."

Mi-jeong pretended to aim a kick at Min-yeong.

"You can do that, or anything else you like, if you want to see me killed off!"

"That's no joke."

"I know, I know. I'm not joking either."

Mi-jeong smiled bitterly, raised her voice and changed the subject.

"What's for breakfast today?"

"Potato soup."

"Make it good. I'll go wake up our kitchen-duty members."

Min-yeong parted from Mi-jeong and headed for the canteen.

They couldn't figure out what was wrong, but the multi-layered steam cooker refused to work, so they would have to make do with bread for breakfast. Min-yeong scoured the neighborhood around the factory to find enough bread, while Sang-rye and Geum-ju prowled about the cooker until she got

연탄난로에 달라붙어 언 손을 녹이고 있던 상례가 경자의 뒤통수에다 욕설을 퍼부었다.

"남이야 버리든 말든. 내 몫 내가 버리는데 왜 잔소리야?"

"처먹고 싸우라고 도와준 거지 버리라고 없는 주머니 털어준 줄 알아?"

"그럼 처먹을 수 있도록 해줘야 할 거 아냐."

"누가 밥하기 싫어서 안 했어야. 기계가 고장인 걸 어떻게 해."

상례와 같이 식사당번인 금주가 전라도 사투리로 가세했다.

민영도 상례나 금주와 마찬가지로 조합원들이 야속했다. 매일 새벽 잠을 설치며 식사를 준비해왔는데 한 끼가 잘못됐다고 모두 싸늘한 눈길만 던질 뿐이었다. 빈말이라도 감싸주는 이 하나 없었다. 배수 밸브가 터지는 바람에 상례는 옷까지 몽땅 버렸다.

개, 소, 돼지, 살쾡이, 셋의 욕설이 뒤엉키고 머리채를 휘어잡기 직전까지 갔다.

"관두지 못해."

민영이 바락 악을 썼다.

back.

December had come by now, which brought cold winds. The 107th day of the strike had come, and difficulties were increasing. The ever-colder weather had brought the mercury down to minus ten degrees Celsius that morning. It had been below freezing for several days in a row now, and the union members had nothing but their own body heat to keep them warm. It was hard to find someone who hadn't caught a cold. Those student members who had been unable to pay the last quarter's tuition had stopped attending school two days before. Yun-hui had left that morning, and now the kitchen stove had broken down.

Min-yeong couldn't look her colleagues in the eye as they walked into the canteen. As usual, they came in asking her what was on the menu with the same slightly apologetic expression on their faces, but when they saw the bread at the serving-hatch, their expressions hardened. They had spent the night shivering from cold, and had come down looking forward to some hot soup at least.

Their expressions were colder than the weather as they accepted their four slices per person. They watched Min-yeong from the corner of their eyes as

경자가 부은 볼을 하고 식당을 나갔다. 표정 없이 싸움을 지켜보던 다른 조합원들도 자리에서 일어섰다. 모두 다 이 정도의 다툼에는 이력이 나 있었다. 식당은 금방 텅 비었다. 식탁 위엔 임자를 잃은 식빵들만 남아 있었다.

민영도 식당을 뛰쳐나왔다. 왜 우리끼리 이래야 하나. 서로 감싸고 다독거려야 할 우리까지 발톱을 세우고 할퀴려 들어야 하나.

하늘은 금방 눈송이라도 내릴 것처럼 잔뜩 찌푸려 있었다.

민영은 기숙사에 들어가 이불을 뒤집어쓰고 누웠다. 순옥은 제 방으로 돌아가 틀어박혔는지 보이지 않았다.

할 만큼은 했다. 나도 더는 어쩔 수 없다. 어떻게 하면 조금이라도 잘 먹일 수 있을까를 온종일 고민하며 지내왔다. 민영의 머릿속에는 온갖 생각이 교차했다. 그러나 그것도 잠깐이었다. 자신도 모르게 스르르 잠으로 빠져들었다. 냉방이었지만 이불 속에 들어가자 새벽내 언 몸이 풀리며 잠이 쏟아졌다.

민영이 애초에 조합에서 맡은 일은 회계감사였다. 2차 농성이 시작되면서 취사부장이 그의 임무로 추가되었다. 200여 명이 넘는 인원의 식사를 감당하기란 쉬운 일이 아

they ventured a couple of bites at the bread before leaving. Some even threw theirs straight into the waste-bin without so much as tasting them.

"We're supposed to eat this stuff?"

Gyeong-ja protested as she dropped her share into the bin.

The union members, exhausted from the long sit-in, had grown as prickly as thorns. Throughout their struggle, there had not been a single place in the world that would offer them a warm welcome.

Hostility. Confronted at every turn with the stout walls of the wealthy with their power, the strikers' feelings of fury gradually built up as outright hostility. There wasn't a single place where they did not encounter a wall erected in support of the factory owner—not only in the company's head office, but also in the Labor Bureau, the Ministry of Labor, and the political parties. And of course, the police never missed a turn. The anger and hostility, hard to endure, sometimes made them target their colleagues. In the bitter struggle, the union members had lost all sense of kindness and generosity, until there was no room in their hearts for even one companion. As their confidence in eventual victory ebbed away, their once intense solidarity had been

니었다. 민영은 세광의 싸움에서 자신이 기여할 수 있는 유일한 방법이 밥짓는 일인 것처럼 매달렸다. 시장 다녀오는 일을 빼면 온종일을 식당에서 벗어나지 못했다. 날이 갈수록 인원이 줄어들어 취사량도 줄어들었다. 그러나 일은 조금도 덜어지지 않았다. 줄어드는 인원보다 농성자금은 빠르게 바닥을 보이고 있었다. 부식비를 최소로 줄일 수밖에 없었고 식사는 점점 부실해졌다. 추위에 까칠해진 조합원들의 입끝을 따라갈 수는 없었다.

"회계감사, 일어나."

민영은 보지 않아도 누군지 알 수 있었다. 위원장이었다.

"이 녀석, 네가 누웠으면 점심은 어떡하니?"

민영은 대답 대신 이불 속에서 등을 돌려 누웠다. 웅크린 민영의 엉덩이를 미정이 장난스럽게 내려쳤다.

"안 일어날 거야?"

미정은 민영이 덮은 이불을 걷었다. 민영은 웅크린 몸을 새우처럼 더욱 웅크렸다.

"민영아, 여기서 주저앉을 순 없지 않니."

미정이 민영의 어깨 위에 손을 얹어놓았다.

"나보고 더 뭘 어떡하라는 거예요."

누운 채 대답했다.

transformed into mutual jealousy and enmity.

"Bitch. Even if you don't want to eat it, how dare you throw it away!" Sang-rye, who was pressed against the stove in an attempt to defrost her frozen hands, spat her words at Gyeong-ja's turned back.

"It's mine to throw away or not. If I throw away what's mine, why should you complain?"

"That's meant to help you stand up and fight; do you think we have food to spare?"

"Then shouldn't you be giving us something we can eat?"

"You think it's because we're fed up cooking rice? The cooker's broken, that's why."

Geum-ju, on kitchen duty with Sang-rye, spoke up in support of her with a strong Jeolla accent.

Like Sang-rye and Geum ju, Min-ycong too was hurt by the unionists' cold-heartedness. Min-yeong rose at the crack of dawn each day to prepare breakfast, and now, when just one meal had gone wrong, everyone glared coldly at her. No one said so much as a word in her favor. Sang-rye had an additional misfortune, ruining her clothes when the wastewater valve burst.

Bitch. Cow. Pig. Lynx. Their curses mingled, they were on the verge of grabbing one another by the

"너 어젯밤에 윤희, 순옥이 걔들한테 뭐라고 그랬니. 철순일 생각해서라도 힘을 내야 한다고 하지 않았어."

"그럼 애들한테 뭐라고 해요. 이젠 나도 지쳤어요."

민영은 자신이 생각해도 아는 게 너무 없었다. 굳은 의지도 없다. 조합원들의 절반 이상이 떨어져나갈 동안 남아 있는 자신이 이상하다. 남은 조합원들은 신경이 밤송이 같았지만 투지와 신념에 차 있었다. 모두가 투쟁을 통해서 변화하고 새롭게 눈 떠가는 동안 자신은 무지렁이로 밥이나 짓고 있었다.

"너마저 그러면 난 어떡하니."

힘없는 목소리다. 민영은 실눈으로 미정의 옆얼굴을 올려봤다. 초벌 뒤의 도자기 인형처럼 표정이 없다.

"나 울어버리는 거 볼래."

커다란 안경 속의 눈자위는 붉게 충혈되어 정말 울어버릴 것 같다. 민영은 자신의 어깨에 놓인 미정의 손을 당겨 잡으며 자리에서 일어나 앉았다. 민영은 미정의 예전 모습을 확인한 게 반가웠다. 미정은 이 긴 투쟁 속에서 수없는 조합원들의 눈물을 지켜보면서도 운 적이 없다. 단 한 번 철순이 죽었을 때 밤새 눈물을 뿌린 적이 있을 뿐이었다.

hair.

"Cut it out, all of you!" Min-yeong suddenly screamed.

Gyeong-ja left the canteen, cheeks ablaze. The other strikers, who had been watching the quarrel blankly, also got up to leave. They had all become accustomed to that kind of squabble. In a moment, the canteen was empty. All that remained were slices of bread on the tables, abandoned by their owners.

Min-yeong also went rushing out of the canteen. *Why does it have to be like this among us? Surely we should be protecting each other and collaborating together instead of baring our claws, ready to scratch one another?*

The sky was darkening as though it was about to snow.

Min-yeong went back to the dormitory and lay down under her blanket. Sun-ok was nowhere to be seen; she was probably holed up back in her own room.

I've done my best. There's nothing more I can do. I spent the entire day trying to figure out how I could feed them a bit better. Min-yeong's head was spinning with all kinds of thoughts. But only for a

승리의 꽃다발을 철순의 무덤 앞에 바치는 그날까지 우린 울어선 안 돼, 우리에겐 아직 울 권리가 없는 거야. 미정의 그 말은 더 큰소리로 조합원들을 울게 만들었지만 자신은 눈물을 보이지 않았다. 다른 조합원들은 미정의 흔들림 없는 표정에서 평온과 용기를 얻었지만 민영은 두터운 벽을 느꼈다. 노조를 만든 뒤 미정은 너무도 빠르게 변해갔다. 옛날의 허물없던 그녀가 아니었다.

미정과 민영은 세광에서 가장 고참이었다. 중학교를 졸업하고 세광에 발 디딘 민영의 나이 지금 스물넷이다. 그보다 한 해 먼저 세광 창립과 함께 입사한 미정의 나이 지금 스물아홉이다. 민영과 미정이 7~8년을 다니는 동안 줄잡아 수천 명이 세광을 거쳐갔다. 어쩌면 만 명이 넘을지도 모른다. 전자는 물론 봉제보다도 약한 일당과 고열, 신나와 안료 냄새 자욱한 도자기 공장을 자신의 평생 일터로 여기는 사람은 없었다. 석 달이 멀다 하고 다른 직장을 찾아 떠나갔고 공단 구인란과 수위실엔 일 년 내내 세광의 모집공고가 붙어 있었다.

수많은 사람들이 들어오고 나가는 동안 미정과 민영은 세광을 지켜왔다. 처음 시작할 땐 하나뿐이던 건물은 다섯 동으로 늘었고 6기뿐이던 가마도 20기로 늘었다. 생산

moment. She was asleep before she knew it. The room was frigid, but once under the blanket her frozen body melted and she fell asleep.

Min-yeong's first job in the union had been as auditor. When the second strike began, she became head cook as well. It wasn't easy being responsible for the meals of over two hundred people. But she clung to her cooking as if it was the only way she could contribute to the struggle. Except when she went shopping for food, she spent all her days in the dining hall. As time went by there were less and less strikers, and less and less food. But there was never any less work. The strike fund was reaching the bottom faster than people were leaving. Her only option was to cut down on food costs, and the meals became increasingly skimpy. She could not match the needs of the unionists, emaciated by the cold.

"Auditor, wake up."

She knew who was speaking without opening her eyes. It was the Chief.

"Lazy bum. What are we supposed to do about lunch with you sleeping here?"

Instead of replying, Min-yeong stayed lying under the blanket, her back turned. Mi-jeong gave curled-

직 사원도 70명에서 300명을 넘어섰다. 해가 가도 불지 않는 것은 얇은 월급봉투뿐이었다. 얼굴을 익히고 친해질 만하면 사람들은 세광을 떠났다. 시간이 지나며 아예 친구 사귀기를 포기했다. 자연 미정은 민영과 가까웠다. 그리고 둘은 관리자들과도 가까웠다.

노조를 만들기 전까지만 해도 미정은 민영과 친자매처럼 가까웠다. 쉬는 시간이면 같이 자판기 커피를 뽑아 마시고 어쩌다 잔업이 없는 날엔 공단 시장으로 순대를 먹으러 다녔다. 미정의 전세방에서 과자 부스러기를 쪼아먹으며 관리자들을 욕하고 동료들을 흉보며 밤을 밝힌 날도 한두 번이 아니다. 그러나 지금 미정은 모든 조합원들의 위원장이 되었다. 민영은 다만 조합원 중의 한 명에 불과했다. 시간이 지날수록 미정과의 사이에 높은 담이 쌓여갔다. 미정은 항상 얼굴에서 웃음을 잃지 않았고 목소리는 자신에 차 있었다.

오랜만에 들어보는 미정의 꾸밈없는 목소리가 반가웠다.

"지금 몇 시야?"

"열한 시 십 분."

"수리기사가 다녀갔는데 수리비용이 이십만 원이라구

up Min-yeong's behind a playful pat.

"Aren't you going to get up?"

Mi-jeong pulled Min-yeong's blanket aside. Min-yeong curled up even more tightly, like a shrimp.

"Min-yeong, we can't give up at this stage."

Mi-jeong placed one hand on Min-yeong's shoulder.

"What more do you expect me to do?"

She answered still lying down.

"What did you tell Yun-hui and Sun-ok last night? Didn't you tell them to remember Cheol-sun and be strong?"

"I had to tell them something. Now I'm worn out."

Min-yeong felt there was nothing she knew. She had never had strong will power, either. It was quite strange that she had stayed on so long, while more than half the strikers had left. Those who had stuck it out might be as prickly as chestnut burrs, but they were still full of fight and conviction. While the struggle had been transforming them and opening their eyes, she had been cooking away like a moron.

"If *you're* like this, whom can I turn to?"

Her voice sounded weak. Min-yeong squinted up at Mi-jeong. Her face was as expressionless as a

해.”

“이십만 원이나 있어요?”

“어떻게 해봐야지.”

위원장은 대수롭지 않은 일처럼 대꾸했다.

“어떻게요. 수리비 이십만 원뿐인가요? 순옥이 등록금 그리고 등록금 내야 할 게 순옥이뿐이에요? 삼십 명 칠만 원씩 이백십만 원. 또 김장 못 한 일반들 김장값, 부식비도 이틀 치밖에 안 남았어요.”

민영은 마치 농성자금이 바닥난 게 미정의 잘못인 것처럼 쏟아부었다. 숨도 쉬지 않고 퍼부어대는 민영의 얼굴을 미정은 애매한 웃음으로 쳐다봤다.

“지금 웃음이 나와요? 위원장님.”

“아니면 울랴.”

“……”

“어쨌든 일어나봐. 굶고 앉았을 순 없잖아.”

“굶고 앉았지 않으면, 누가 공짜로 돈 준대?”

“그래 준댄다.”

미정이 무릎을 감싸고 쪼그려앉은 민영을 일으켜 세웠다.

“어디 가려고.”

newly made porcelain doll's.

"Do you want to see me break down in tears?"

Her eyes, bloodshot behind her enormous glasses, certainly looked as if they were about to burst into tears at any moment. Min-yeong took the hand that Mi-jeong had placed on her shoulder and pulled herself up to a sitting position. Min-yeong was happy to find Mi-jeong the same as she had been before. During the long struggle, Mi-jeong had witnessed the tears of countless unionists, but she had never cried herself. The only time she had cried was when Cheol-sun died; then she had wept all night long.

Until the day when we lay a victory wreath on Cheol-sun's grave we must not cry; we have no right to cry till then. Mi-jeong's words had made all the unionists cry even more, but she herself shed no tears. The other unionists had been filled with peace and courage by Mi-jeong's determined expression, but Min-yeong felt a thick wall. After establishing the labor union, Mi-jeong had quickly changed. She was no longer the open, friendly woman she had before been.

Mi-jeong and Min-yeong were the most senior in the factory. Min-yeong had started working at

"가보면 알아."

미정은 막무가내로 민영의 팔을 잡아끌었다.

"머리도 안 감았단 말야."

"그냥도 충분히 예뻐. 밖에 눈도 와."

기숙사 복도를 지나는 동안 곳곳에서 라면 끓이는 냄새가 풍겨나왔다. 민영은 비로소 허기를 느꼈다.

"정말 눈이잖아?"

새벽부터 잔뜩 찌푸렸던 하늘에선 눈송이가 흩날렸다. 정문을 나선 둘은 팔짱을 끼고 나란히 걸었다.

"선홍정밀 가려고 그러지?"

"잘 아네."

"갈 데가 뻔하지 뭐."

2

똥바다의 둑방길을 따라 걷는 두 사람의 머리와 어깨 위로 눈이 얹혔다.

시커멓게 누운 개펄로 바닷물이 차오르고 있었다. 개펄 양켠의 대형 하수구에서는 쉼없이 폐수가 흘러나왔다. 바닷물과 폐수가 뒤섞인 똥바다는 가는 물결로 일렁거렸다.

Segwang after graduating from middle school, and was now twenty-four years old. Mi-jeong had started a year before that, when the factory was established, and was now twenty-nine. In the seven or eight years when the two had been in the factory, thousands of workers had come and gone, at a modest estimate. Maybe it had been more than ten thousand. No one thought of working a whole lifetime in a ceramics factory, with daily wages less than for needlework, not to mention electronics. The heat and the overbearing stench of thinner and pigments were unbearable, too. Most people went to look for other jobs after less than three months. Segwang's recruiting advertisements were pasted up across the industrial complex and in the factory gatehouse twelve months a year.

While crowds came to Segwang and left again, Mi-jeong and Min-yeong stayed faithful. When they started working there, the factory consisted of one building only; now there were five, and the number of kilns also grew from six to twenty. The number of productive workers also increased from seventy to over three hundred. The only thing that never seemed to expand from year to year was the thin envelope that contained the wages. People would

그 물결 위로도 함박눈이 내려앉고 있었다.

작업 시간의 공단은 기계 소리만 요란했다. 거리에는 인적이 끊겼다. 아무에게도 밟히지 않은 채 고스란히 쌓여가는 눈길을 두 사람은 발자국을 찍으며 지나갔다. 이 길을 따라 선홍정밀로 가려면 공단을 온전히 한 바퀴 도는 셈이 된다.

"지금도 갈매기가 있을까요?"

"지난봄의 그 갈매기들…… 있겠지."

"이렇게 날씨가 추운데."

"갈매기는 제비가 아니잖아."

미정은 발이 시렸다. 낡은 운동화 사이로 스며든 물기가 발바닥을 적셨다. 서로의 주머니에 바꿔 찌른 손도 마찬가지로 시렸다.

"마석에도 눈이 내릴까?"

민영이 남은 한 손으로 머리 위에 쌓인 눈송이를 털어냈다.

"글쎄."

"철순이도 춥겠지."

"하얀 눈이불을 덮으면 포근할 거야."

"언니, 철순이 보고 싶지 않아?"

leave Segwang just as they got to recognize their faces or to know them. With time, the two stopped trying to make friends. Naturally, Mi-jeong grew close to Min-yeong. And the two grew close to the administrators.

Until the creation of the union, Mi-jeong and Min-yeong were closer than blood sisters. At every break, they would drink coffee together that they got from the vending machine, and if ever they weren't working overtime, they would head for the local market to feast on sausages. The two spent many a night in Mi-jeong's rented room, snacking on cookie crumbs, badmouthing the administrators, and gossiping about fellow workers. But now Mi-jeong had become the leader of the employees' union, while Min-yeong was just another employee. As time passed, a high wall arose between her and Mi-jeong. Mi-jeong never lost the smile on her face, and her voice always brimmed with confidence.

The unaccustomed sound of Mi-jeong's long-lost natural voice made her feel glad.

"What time is it?"

"Eleven-ten."

"The repairman was here. He said the repairs would cost 200,000 *won.*"

"왜, 여기 오니까 옛날 생각 나?"

"그땐 참 한심했지, 왜 싸웠는지 몰라."

"민영아, 우리 다시 갈매기 찾기 할까. 다섯 마리 먼저 찾기."

"그때처럼 자장면 사기."

"그래, 싸움 끝나면 먹기로 하고."

철순은 미정, 민영과 함께 세우회의 회원이었다. 미정은 페인팅실의 조장이었고 철순과 민영은 화공부의 조장이었다.

세우회는 현장 조장들로부터 과장까지 생산라인의 친목회였다. 월급날이면 회비를 떼어 회식하는 게 주된 활동이었다. 갈비집에서부터 시작하여 스탠드바까지 몰려다니며 목의 때를 벗겼다. 어쩌다 연안부두의 횟집까지 진출하기도 했다. 부족한 비용은 회사가 냈다. 과장은 빠뜨리지 않고 영수증을 떼었다.

세우회의 회원들은 자신들끼리만 어울렸고 현장 동료들과는 자연 거리가 있었다. 현장 동료들의 눈에는 좋게 보일 리 없었다. 현장의 사정보다는 회사의 입장을 앞세우는 회원들을 달갑게 여기는 사람들은 사장과 관리자들뿐이었다.

"Do we have that much money?"

"We just have to find it."

Mi-jeong responded as if it was a trivial matter.

"But what are we to do? It's not just the 200,000 *won* for repairs, is it? There's Sun-ok's tuition, and not only hers, either. We've got thirty people with tuitions of 70,000 *won* each—that's two million one hundred thousand *won*. There's the cost of providing winter kimchi for everyone who can't make their own, and there's only enough money for two days' food supplies."

Min-yeong's words poured out as if Mi-jeong was to blame for the fact that their strike fund had almost run out. Mi-jeong looked at Min-yeong's face with an ambiguous smile while she rattled on, not pausing for breath.

"Chief, really. This is no laughing matter."

"Should I cry instead?"

Min-yeong said nothing.

"Anyway, try to stand up. There's no point in starving sitting down, is there?"

"And if I don't starve sitting here—will someone give us money for free?"

"They might, you know."

Mi-jeong helped Min-yeong up from where she

철순은 세우회의 예외적인 존재였다. 늘 주위엔 동료들이 모여들었다. 관리자들의 따가운 시선에도 아랑곳 않고 현장 동료들과 허물없이 지냈다. '좋은 게 좋은' 세우회의 분위기를 흐려놓는 것도 철순이었다. 현장 동료들의 처지를 염두해 두지 않는 회사 측의 처사를 들고 나와 화기애애한 분위기에 초를 치기가 일쑤였다. 해줄 거 해주고 시킬 거 시켜라, 가 그녀의 주의였다. 현장 동료들에겐 단연 인기였다. 관리자들의 눈밖에 나는 만큼 반비례하여. 민영도 자신의 불만을 주저없이 토로하는 철순이 싫지 않았다. 그렇다고 이제 입사 3년밖에 되지 않은 그녀가 자신과 같은 위치에 서로 동료들의 인기를 독차지하는 게 기꺼울 수는 없었다. 특히나 같은 부서에서 조장을 맡고 있는 둘은 여러모로 비교될 수밖에 없었다.

철순과 민영의 사이에 명확한 정대관계가 형성된 것은 부서가 분리되고부터였다. 회사는 올해 초 공정의 합리화와 기동성 있는 제품의 생산이라는 기치를 내걸고 기존의 생산라인을 완전히 둘로 분리했다. 제토, 소성, 성형, 제형, 화공, 페인팅, 포장으로 구성된 부서를 제토와 포장만을 제외하고는 반씩 둘로 나누었다. 화공부서도 화공 1부와 화공 2부로 나누어졌다. 민영과 철순은 1부와 2부의

was huddled hugging her knees.

"Where are we going?"

"You'll see."

Mi-jeong took her firmly by the arm.

"Why, I haven't even washed my hair."

"You look pretty enough as you are. Besides, it's snowing out there."

As they passed through the dormitory corridors, they were met by the rich smell of instant noodles coming from every room. Min-yeong suddenly felt famished.

"It really is snowing!"

The sky, which had been overcast since early morning, was now full of dancing snowflakes. The two locked arms and strode out of the front gate.

"We're going to Seonheung Precision Mechanics, aren't we?"

"How did you know?"

"It's the obvious place to go, surely?"

2

The snow settled on the head and shoulders of the two women walking along the edge of the Shit Sea.

조장으로 임명되었다.

부서 분리의 이유를 회사는 다양한 품목을 신속하게 생산하기 위한 것이라고 했다. 사실과는 거리가 멀었다. 그것은 며칠 지나지 않아서 명확하게 드러났다. 둘로 분리된 라인에 동일한 제품이 투입되었다. 그 결과는 서로 비교되지 않을 수 없었다. 한쪽에는 격려와 치하가, 또 한쪽에는 추궁과 압박의 살아 있는 근거가 되었다.

치열한 경쟁을 피할 수 없었다.

민영의 라인은 점심시간까지 죽여가며 수량을 뽑아냈다. 철순의 화공 2부는 지시량조차 채우지 못했다.

작업지시가 떨어지는 조회시간마다 철순은 호된 질책을 감당해야 했다. 라인 분리 전 지시량과 생산량을 현재와 비교하며 철순이 항변했지만 조금도 먹혀들지 않았다.

"공정을 합리화했잖아. 수천만 원을 들여 공정을 합리적으로 개선했는데 생산량은 그대로 뽑겠다는 건 무슨 심보야?"

생산과장은 라인 분리에 든 비용을 일일이 열거했다.

"라인을 분리한다고 손이 두 개에서 셋으로 늘어나는 건 아니잖아요. 어차피 똑같은 손으로 똑같은 안료, 똑같이 붓칠하는 건 달라진 게 없잖아요. 우리가 작업하는 데

The incoming tide had started to cover the dark mudflats. Wastewater flowed ceaselessly out through the large sewers at the two ends of the mudflats. The Shit Sea, where seawater and wastewater mingled, was tossed by small waves. The snow was even settling on the waves.

This being working hours, the industrial complex was loud with the noise of machines. There wasn't a soul in the streets. The snow remained undisturbed on the ground except for the footprints left by the two women. To reach Seonheung Precision Mechanics by the road they were taking would mean making a complete turn of the complex.

"Do you think the seagulls are still around?"

"The ones from last spring...? They should be."

"But it's so cold."

"Gulls are not swallows, you know."

Mi-jeong's toes were freezing. The moisture seeping into her old sneakers was soaking the soles of her feet. Their fingers, which they took turns warming up in each other's pockets, were equally cold.

"Do you think it's snowing in Maseok too?"

Min-yeong used her free hand to dust off the snow from her hair.

"I'm not sure."

서 변한 건 아무것도 없어요. 지시량 는 것 빼고는요."

철순이 당돌하게 대들었지만 과장은 한마디로 일축했다.

"너 계속 똑똑한 체하는데, 화공 1부는 그럼 어떻게 지시량을 넘겨 뽑았어. 걔네들은 손이 세 개로 늘어났어?"

과장은 민영과 철순을 번갈아 봤다. 그러고는 한마디를 덧붙였다.

"조장이 그러니 그 모양인 거 아냐?"

두 부서의 평균 생산량이 표준량으로 정해졌다. 지시량은 그보다도 많은 최고 생산량을 기준으로 떨어졌다. 주가 바뀔 때마다 표준량과 지시량은 올라갔다. 철순의 화공 2부도 생산량이 조금씩 늘어났지만 지시량은 더 많은 폭으로 증가했다. 민영의 1부서도 더이상 증가가 불가능할 때쯤이면 다른 제품이 투입되어왔다. 그리고 똑같은 과정이 되풀이되었다.

화공 1부는 게으른 2부 때문에 자신들의 몫이 늘어난다고 눈을 흘겼다. 2부는 또 미련한 1부 때문에 지시량이 고무줄처럼 늘어난다고 이를 갈았다. 점심시간 공놀이조차 하지 않았다. 엉뚱하게도, 자신의 살을 갉아먹도록 강요하는 사슬을 어떻게 끊어야 하는지 모르는 부서원들은 서

"Cheol-sun's probably freezing, too."

"She's probably snug under a thick blanket of snow."

"Don't you miss Cheol-sun, Eonni[1]?"

"Why, is coming here making you remember old times?"

"It was so pathetic. I don't know why we got into that fight."

"C'mon, Min-yeong, let's look for seagulls. The first to spot five, wins."

"And the loser has to treat the winner with black bean *jajang* noodles, just like last time."

"Okay. We'll eat them after the strike's over."

Cheol-sun had been a member of the same social club as Mi-jeong and Min-yeong. Mi-jeong was in charge of the painting room, and Cheol-sun and Min-yeong were in charge of the chemical processing section.

The Segwang Fraternity Club was a social association intended to promote friendship among production-line employees from section head up to department head level. Its main activity was collecting membership fees every month on payday and using that money for a party. It was always a full-blown celebration, starting in a barbecue house and end-

로에게 발톱을 드러내고 으르렁거렸다.

민영과 철순이 정면으로 부딪친 것은 조회시간이었다. 점심시간을 죽이고 쉬는 시간을 건너뛰는 것도 하루이틀이지 화공 1부라고 불만이 터져나오지 않을 수 없었다.

"오늘 또 지시량을 올려잡으면 어떡하라는 거예요."

민영은 항의했다.

"위에서야 전체 수량을 보고 잡는 거니까 1부로서는 좀 억울하더라도 어쩔 수 없지."

민영은 철순을 노려봤다. 야, 니들 도대체 어떡할 거야. 철순은 대답도 표정도 없이 민영을 마주 쳐다보기만 했다.

"니들 도대체 언제까지 개길 거냐니깐."

"지금까지 지시량 끌어올린 게 누군데 그래. 왜 끝까지 책임지지 못해?"

"나 땜이란 말야, 지금?"

"아니면."

이 뚝방에서 민영과 철순이 만난 것은 그날 저녁이었다. 둘은 잔업도 않고 나왔다. 너 이따 저녁에 좀 봐. 민영이 먼저였다. 누가 겁날 줄 알고. 철순도 피하지 않았다. 좋아, 똥바다에서 만나자.

ing in a bar. There were occasions when they even went to a sushi restaurant on the quay. Whatever amount was lacking would be paid by the company. The department manager invariably saved the receipts.

The members of the club only hung out with other members, so naturally there was some distance between them and their fellow workers working at the factory. In these other workers' eyes they did not look so good. The only people satisfied with the organization's members, who seemed to give precedence to the company's viewpoint rather than the situation in the factory, were the president and administrators.

Cheol-sun was an exception among the club's members. Other workers always flocked around her. She was on familiar terms with them, ignoring the sharp glances of the administrators. And it was Cheol-sun who cast a shadow over the 'happy happy' club meetings. She would bring up the management's indifference to the situation of the workers and spoil the pleasant atmosphere. Her principle was always: Do right by the workers, and then give them orders. So she was definitely popular with the workers, and to a corresponding degree unpopular

민영으로서는 한바탕 단단히 할 작정이었다. 그러나 철순의 태도는 뜻밖이었다. 일전을 불사할 것 같던 아침과는 완전히 달라져 있었다.

"미안해, 너한테 화낼 일이 아닌데 그랬어."

민영은 얘가 왜 이러나 싶었다.

"사람들은 다 알고 있잖아. 너도 알고 있고. 왜 지시량이 늘어나는지, 무엇 때문인지."

철순은 말을 멈추고 건너편 8공단을 건너봤다. 검붉은 노을이 공장 지붕과 굴뚝 사이로 물들고 있었다.

"사람들은 두려운 거야. 회사와 다투기엔 엄두도 나지 않고."

화해를 붙일 양으로 따라나온 미정도 묵묵히 8공단을 건너봤다. 한결같이 칙칙한 회색빛 건물들이었다.

"미정 언니, 8년 다녀서 지금 일당 얼마야? 사천이백십 원. 뭐가 남았어요? 내년, 내후년이면 나아질까? 이게 우리들의 현실이야. 그런데 그것도 모자라서 우리끼리 싸워야 하는 거야? 언닌, 너무 비참하단 생각 안 들어?"

철순은 혼자 묻고 대답했다. 철순의 부서에선 경쟁이 없어진 게 아니었다. 오히려 보이지 않는 내부의 경쟁이 더욱 치열하게 진행되었다. 자신의 부서가 1부보다 수량

with the management. Min-yeong felt no dislike for Cheol-sun, who never hesitated to express her complaints. At the same time, Min-yeong couldn't feel happy at the way this woman, who held the same position as she did even after being in the company for three short years, monopolized popularity among their colleagues. In addition, since the two of them worked at the same station and had the same responsibilities, they were bound to be compared with one other.

It was after their section was divided into two that the two became real rivals. Under the banner of process rationalization and more flexible mobilization of production, at the start of that year the company had split each existing production line into two. What until then had been one unit consisting of Clay-Preparation, Plastic Clay, Molding, Forms, Chemicals, Painting, and Packaging, was divided neatly into two, with the exception of Clay-Preparation and Packaging. The Chemicals section was divided into Chemicals 1 and Chemicals 2, with Min-yeong and Cheol-sun at the head of each.

The reason for the division, they were told, was to speed up the production of a wide variety of articles. But this was far from the truth. That became

을 적게 뽑는다는 건 너무나 명확했다. 부서원들은 적어도 그 책임이 자신에게 있지 않음을 입증해야 했다. 하지만 겉으로는 속내를 보이지 말아야 했다. 옆사람보다는 단 하나만이라도 더 뽑아야 했다. 살을 말리는 경쟁이었다. 차라리 아니꼽더라도 1부와 경쟁을 하는 게 나았을 것이다. 모든 부서원이 하나하나 경쟁자이지는 않았을 것이다. 철순을 아프게 하는 것은 동료들이 끝내 결별하지 못하는 뿌리 깊게 길들여진 경쟁이었다. 그녀가 감당하지 못하는 것은 과장의 질책이나, 민영보다 자신이 무능하다는 비교가 아니었다.

뚝방에 걸터앉은 셋에게 퇴근길의 남성 노동자들이 휘파람을 보냈다. 뚝방 곳곳은 소주병을 가운데 놓고 술판을 벌이는 사람들로 시끄러웠다. 미정 일행의 가까이에서도 슬레이트 조각에 돼지고기를 굽는 패거리들이 시끄럽게 떠들어댔다.

"나, 뭐가 남았냐구? 많지. 자기 공장 7년에 만성두통, 신경통, 소화불량, 위장병. 이 정도면 많이 남은 거 아냐?"

미정은 자신을 비웃었다.

"그래도 편안하니까 다니는 거야. 다른 데 가봐야 특별히 뾰족한 수도 없고."

clear within a few days. The same items were assigned to each subsection. The result, inevitably, was that they were then compared. The effective outcome was that one side received encouragement and appreciation, while the other endured criticism and coercion.

Inevitably, that meant cutthroat competition.

Min-yeong's production line would work all through lunchtime, pumping out vast quantities. Cheol-sun's section failed to fulfill their assigned quotas.

At every morning gathering where the day's quotas were assigned, Cheol-sun had to endure severe reproaches. She protested, comparing the current quotas and production volumes with those before the division of the lines, but the protest got her nowhere.

"We rationalized the process, didn't we? We spent tens of millions of *won* on rationalizing the process; so how dare you say you're going to maintain the same production rates as before?"

The production manager was always specifying just how much the division of the production line had cost.

"Just because the line was divided doesn't mean

미정은 세광에서, 적어도 생산직 노동자 중에서 가장 많은 자유를 누렸다. 300여 명 중에서 매월 생리휴가를 찾아먹는 유일한 사람이었고, 월차를 쓰고 싶은 날 쓰는 것도 그녀 외에는 없었다. 사람들은 창립 멤버니까 어련히 그런가보다 했다. 과장, 부장들과도 농담을 거리낌없이 주고받고 심지어 사장과도 웃음을 터뜨려가며 얘기를 할 정도였다. 중간관리자들도 어설프게 미정을 건드렸다가는 본전 건지기 힘들었다.

그러나 미정의 그러한 자유와 위치를 보장하는 것은 무엇보다도 그녀의 페인팅 기술이었다. 공장 창립과 더불어 온갖 시행착오를 겪으며 단련되어온 그녀의 페인팅 기술은 그 누구도 넘볼 수 없었다. 페인팅에 관한 한 그녀는 도사로 통했다. 저거 홍콩에서 되돌아온다, 하면 틀림없이 클레임이 걸려 되돌아왔고 현장은 비상이 걸렸다. 안료 배합 비율과 도색 두께, 건조 온도 등에 대한 표준서가 그녀에게는 필요없었다. 그녀의 손이 저울이고 눈이 컬러 분석기였다.

"그런데 왜 페인팅실에선 조용해?"

둘로 분리된 부서 중에서 서로 알력이 없는 곳은 페인팅실이 유일했다.

we have three hands each instead of two. We're using the same number of hands and the same pigments, painting with the same gestures, so nothing has changed, has it? There's been no change in the way we work. Except for the increased quotas."

Cheol-sun stood her ground boldly, but the manager cut her down in a flash.

"You think you're so smart, but why is it, then, that Chemicals Team One is able to exceed their quotas? Have they grown an extra hand each?"

The manager looked back and forth between Min-yeong and Cheol-sun.

"It looks as though it depends on the team leader, doesn't it?"

The average production rate of the two teams had been fixed as the standard for both. Quotas were based on the higher production rate. Production rates and quotas increased week after week. Cheol-sun's section increased their production rate slightly, but their quota rose more rapidly. Every time Min-yeong's team reached its absolute limit, another product was added. Then the same process started all over again.

Team One kept giving Team Two dirty looks, reckoning that their share had increased because of

"내가 있는데 감히 무슨 일이 일어날 수 있겠어."

미정이 허풍스럽게 자신의 가슴을 가리켰다.

"야이, 헛똑똑이들아. 싸우고 말고 할 게 뭐 있니. 철순이 얘도 입만 발랐지 헛거야. 짜면 되잖아. 얼마나씩 뽑을 건지. 우리 작업일지 봐. 매일 10개에서 15개 이상 차이 안 나게 2실에서 적게 뽑지. 나보다 지들이 많이 뽑아선 안 되잖아. 1주일에 하루씩만 우리가 걔들보다 적게 뽑지. 그것만으로도 걔들한텐 칭찬거리지. 그러니 뭐가 문제냐. 이것들아. 히프를 굴려라, 히프를."

미정은 둘의 머리를 쿡쿡 찔렀다.

"우리한테도 좀 알려주면 어디 덧나요?"

둘의 얘기를 듣고만 있던 민영이 처음으로 입을 열었다.

"공장밥을 몇 년씩 먹은 것들이 그 정도 통밥도 안 돌아? 수량 적다고 뭐라고 그러면 미친 척하고 불량 잔뜩 뽑아놓고 그래 봐."

"머리가 나쁘면 평생 고생이라니까."

셋은 웃음을 터뜨렸다.

"하지만 통밥이 모자라서만은 아냐. 우리도 그 정도 짱구야 굴리지. 페인팅실이 각본대로 움직이는 건 미정 언

Team Two's laziness. For their part, Team Two ground their teeth in frustration as they watched the quotas stretch like elastic day after day, thanks to Team One's dimwittedness. They didn't even play ball during their lunch break. Unable to find a way of breaking the chains cutting into their flesh, the team members bared their claws and quarreled.

Min-yeong and Cheol-sun finally clashed head on at a morning gathering. Dissatisfaction at the way Team One had been skipping lunch and rest breaks all that time was bound to emerge sooner or later.

"If the production quota goes up again today, how are we to manage?" Min-yeong protested.

"It's been decided up there on the basis of the total production—it may seem unfair to Team One, but you'll just have to accept it" was the response Min-yeong received.

Min-yeong glared at Cheol-sun as if to say: *Hey, what the hell are you going to do about it?* Without a word, Cheol-sun simply looked at Min-yeong expressionlessly.

"How long are you lot going to drag your feet like this?" asked Min-yeong.

"Whose fault is it if quotas keep increasing like this? Shouldn't you take responsibility for what

니가 있으니까 되지, 우린 달라."

민영도 맞장구를 쳤다.

"우리끼리 짜도 과장님이 와서 작업 속도가 왜 이렇게 안 나느냐고 한마디만 하면 손들이 대번 빨라질 걸."

힘이 없을 때 경쟁을 피할 수 없다. 페인팅실은 미정의 무시할 수 없는 힘이 경쟁을 막아내고 있다. 철순은 자신의 부서원들이 왜 경쟁을 포기하지 못하는지를 번쩍 깨달았다. 힘, 힘이었다. 자신은 부서원들의 힘 있는 방패막이가 되어주지 못하는 것이다. 수량이 떨어지는 책임을 부서원 개개인이 직접 져야 했다.

"니들이 만만하게 보이니까 그런 거야. 왜 계장, 주임 따위가 라인작업에까지 간섭하니, 니들을 물로 본다는 거 아냐."

"그건 그래."

"야, 우리 내일 셋 다 제껴버리자."

미정의 갑작스런 제안이었다.

"셋 다 없으면 어떻게 되나 한번 보는 거야. 우선 너희들 말발부터 세워. 그래야 니들한테도 함부로 못한다고."

"회사에서 가만있을까."

민영은 엄두가 나지 않는 모양이었다.

you've been doing?"

"Are you're saying it's *my* fault?"

"Who else's?"

Their meeting on the embankment took place that evening. The two had left work without doing overtime. Meet me tonight: Min-yeong had spoken first. "You think I'm scared?" Cheol-sun had accepted. "Fine, we'll meet by the Shit Sea."

Min-yeong was determined to lay it out squarely. But Cheol-sun's attitude took her by surprise. It was quite different from that morning, when she seemed to be determined to pick a fight.

"Look, I'm sorry. It's not you I should be angry with."

Min-yeong wondered what she meant.

"Everyone knows. You know, too. Just why the quotas have been increasing like they have."

Cheol-sun stopped short and looked across at the 8th complex. The dark-red twilight was shining on the rooftops and between the chimneys.

"It's because people are scared. They just don't have the guts to confront the company."

Mi-jeong, who had tagged along in the hope of reconciling the two women, also gazed quietly across at the factories.

"가만있지 않으면?"

미정이 되물었다.

"미정 언니하고 우린 다르잖아. 언니야 생리 월차 처리되지만 우린 주차까지 네 개가 한꺼번에 날아가잖아."

"병신들아, 누가 못 찾아먹으래, 니들도 한번 붙어서 싸워봐라. 주나 안 주나. 제 밥 제가 찾아먹지 않으면 누가 찾아주냐. 철순이 너도 다른 말을 다 잘하면서 네 생리 월차조차 못 찾아먹는 건 뭐냐."

"나 혼자서만 찾아먹고 싶지 않았어요."

민영은 과장의 얼굴이 먼저 떠올랐다. 항상 따뜻하게 자신을 보살펴준 사람이었다. 그는 민영이 처음 입사했을 때 배치받은 반의 반장이었다. 현장직에서 유일하게 과장까지 올랐기 때문에 세광 노동자들은 그를 자랑으로 여겼다. 그 또한 늘 자신이 현장 출신임을, 그래서 그 누구보다 현장의 사정을 잘 알고 이해하며 애정을 가지고 일한다고 강조해왔다. 그의 그러한 이해가 부서 분리라는 애정 넘치는 아이디어를 사장에게 내놓았다는 걸 민영은 알지 못했다. 그에게 걱정을 끼치는 일을 하고 싶지 않았다. 몇 번이고 세광을 떠나려다 포기한 것도 과장의 설득과 격려가 있었기 때문이었다.

"Look, Mi-jeong Eonni! You've been here for eight years and how much do you make a day? Four thousand two hundred and ten *won*? What have you got left to show for it? Do you think things are going to get better next year, or the year after that? That's our reality! And as if that's not enough, do we have to be fighting among ourselves? Can't we see how grim things are?"

Cheol-sun answered her own questions. It wasn't that her team had lost its competitive spirit. On the contrary, under the surface the competition they were engaged in was fiercer than ever. There was no question that her team was producing less than Team One. Each of her team members had at least to prove that she was not to blame. However, they had to keep their intention hidden. Each of them was obliged to produce just one object more than the person beside her. The competition was draining. There was no need to think long to see that competing with Team One was preferable. Then the members of the team would no longer be one another's rivals. What pained Cheol-sun was the way the spirit of competition was so deeply rooted in her colleagues that it could not be broken. It was neither the department manager's reproaches nor

"내일은 영종도 가서 배나 타다 오자. 모레는 일요일이니까 집에서 푹 쉬고."

미정은 혼자 한발 더 나가고 있었다.

"특근할 텐데."

민영은 아무래도 내키지 않았다.

"야, 니가 왜 건방지게 사장님 걱정을 대신 하니? 사장님도 항상 말씀하시잖아. 분수에 맞는 생활을 하라고."

"선적 날짜도 며칠 안 남았잖아요."

"세광에서 충신 났군. 충신 났어."

쯧쯧, 미정은 혀를 찼다.

"너 개근 못할까 봐 그러지, 아서라 아서."

"그까짓 개근이 뭐 대단하다고 그래."

그렇게 부인하는 민영의 얼굴이 새빨갛게 달아올랐다. 민영은 세광에 다닌 7년 동안 한 번도 결근을 하지 않았다. 아니, 단 한 번 결근한 적이 있긴 했다. 어느 해 여름인가 홍수가 졌을 때였다. 집이 잠겨 도저히 출근할 수가 없었다. 회사 생활 하면서 이런 흠집 남겨선 안 돼, 하며 출근 카드를 고쳐준 것도 지금의 생산과장이었다.

"아니긴 뭐가 아냐. 내가 세광의 터줏귀신이다. 개근 그게 사람 잡는 올가미라는 거야. 때려치우고 싶어도 3년 다

the comparison between her and Min-yeong that she had a problem with.

Male workers whistled at the three women sitting on the embankment as they left work. The embankment grew noisy as groups began to congregate amidst bottles of *soju*. A group that had settled right next to them was cooking pieces of pork on a piece of slate, chattering noisily.

"What have I got to show for it, you ask?" Mi-jeong joked. "Oh, lots. After seven years in a ceramics factory I have a chronic headache, bad nerves, indigestion, stomach disorders. Doesn't that sound like a lot? Still, I feel comfortable here, so I keep going. There's no obviously better job waiting for me elsewhere."

Mi-jeong had the most freedom in the entire factory—at least compared with the other production workers. She was the only one out of three hundred who took a monthly "period day" off from work, and she alone took off one other day a month when she chose. The others simply figured it was because she was one of the factory's founding workers. It went so far that she could exchange jokes with the heads of the section and department, even share a laugh with the owner. And no middle

닌 거 아까워 못하고, 다음에는 4년 개근 아까워 못하고, 4천 원 벌려고 아침 거르고 2천 원어치 택시 타게 만드는 게 개근이라는 거다. 나도 4년 개근했어. 창립기념일날은수저 한 벌이야 아깝겠지만 말야. 종잇조각 하나하고."

"그러지 말고 우리 내일 출근은 하되 잔업을 제껴버리는 게 어떨까."

철순이 새로운 제안을 했다.

"그리고 모레는 쉬고."

미정은 흔쾌히 동의했다.

"애들이야 좋아하겠지만……"

"잔업이야 하고 않는 게 본인 마음대로 아냐. 법에도 다 보장된 건데 뭘."

철순이 머뭇거리는 민영을 부추겼다.

"뭣 때문에 그러는지를 밝혀야 할 거 아네요. 부서 분리 철회, 어때요."

"그래."

셋은 자리를 털고 일어났다. 미정이 둘을 양쪽 팔에 끼고 걸었다. 아직 바닷물이 덜 차오른 개펄 위로 갈매기 몇 마리가 떼지어 서성거리고 있었다. 민영이 짓궂게 돌멩이를 집어던졌다. 다섯 마리의 갈매기가 날아올랐다. 흰색

managers could dare mistreat her.

Still, what really guaranteed Mi-jeong's freedom and position was her superior painting skills. She had been forged by all the trials and errors that came with the establishment of the factory, and no one could match her painting skills. She was considered a master where painting was concerned. If she said of something, "That will come back from Hong Kong," it would surely come back with a claim attached, and the factory would be in a state of emergency. She did not need any books listing the correct ratio of pigments, the right thickness of paint, or the drying temperatures. Her hands were the scale and her eyes the gauge of color.

"But why is it so quiet in the painting room?"

Of all the sections that had been divided, the painting room was the only place where there was no friction.

"It's because I'm there, so nothing could go wrong, could it?"

Mi-jeong pointed at herself with a boastful air.

"Listen, you idiots. There's something better to be done than arguing. Cheol-sun is merely full of talk. Why don't you put your heads together? Decide how many you're going to produce each day! Take

보다는 검은색에 가깝도록 더럽혀진 몸뚱이를 한 갈매기들은 바쁜 날갯짓을 하며 건너 개펄로 옮겨갔다.

"저 갈매기들은 뭘 먹고 살까."

민영이 걱정스럽다는 듯이 중얼거렸다.

"쇳물."

"화공약품 찌꺼기."

미정과 철순의 대꾸를 흘려들으며 민영이 되물었다.

"똥바다엔 물고기도 살지 않을 텐데. 식당에서 버린 짬밥을 먹고 살까."

"짬밥은 돼지 기르는 데서 다 걷어가지 않니. 갈매기는 꿈을 먹고 사는 거야."

미정은 자신의 말에 스스로 웃었다.

"저 갈매기들은 아마 썰물을 따라 나가면 드넓은 바다가 열린다는 걸 모를 거야. 노동자의 운명은 가난과 굴욕이라고 생각하는 우리들처럼 똥바다가 바다의 전부라고 생각할 거야."

"야, 철순이 얘 시 쓰고 있는데."

셋은 공동의 음모를 가슴에 지녀서인지 괜히 들떠서 소리 높여 웃었다. 지나는 사람들이 셋을 쳐다봤다.

7공단과 8공단 사이를 가로지르고 누운 이 개펄을 사람

a look at the daily production records from the painting section. The second team needs to make sure they produce ten or fifteen pieces less than the first every day. They can't attempt to produce more than my team, can they? And once a week we make less than they do. That wins them praise. So what's the problem? You've got to rack your bottoms."

Mi-jeong poked their heads.

"You should have suggested that before."

Min-yeong, who had merely being listening to the other two, finally spoke up.

"C'mon—you've both been in the factory all these years and you still don't get the picture? If they complain you're producing too little, you should produce lots of defective goods as if you've gone crazy."

Mi-jeong continued, "If you're stupid, you're in for a hard time all your life."

The three of them had a good laugh at that.

"It's not just a matter of not getting the picture. We've been using our heads too. Everything runs according to plan in the painting room only because you're there, Mi-jeong Eonni. It's different with us."

Min-yeong chimed in.

"Even if we put our heads together, a manager

들은 똥바다라 불렀다. 만조가 되면 뚝방까지 차오른 바닷물이 출렁거렸다. 물이 빠져 나가는 간조가 되면 시커멓게 더럽혀진 개펄은 흉측스런 등짝을 드러냈다. 개펄 언저리 곳곳엔 밤사이 몰래 버린 공단 폐기물들이 산더미를 이루었다. 버려진 폐수와 오물, 쓰레기들의 썩는 냄새가 소금 냄새와 뒤섞여 코를 찔렀다. 똥바다라 이름하기에 조금도 부족함이 없는 이 개펄의 뚝방을 그래도 갈 곳 없는 공단 사람들은 휴식처로 삼았다.

"우리 갈매기 찾기 하자. 저쪽으로 날아간 다섯 마리 빼고 새로 다섯 마리 찾기."

미정의 얘기에 민영이 내기를 걸었다.

"좋아. 자장면 사기."

미정과 민영은 인천교가 눈에 들어오도록 한 마리의 갈매기도 찾을 수 없었다. 바다가 열리는 서녘 끝으로 개펄을 가로지른 인천교 위로는 차량들이 질주했다.

"그때는 철순이가 자장면 샀는데 오늘은 우리 둘 중에 하나가 걸릴 수밖에 없겠지."

"너무 추워서 어디 다 숨어버린 모양이다 야."

인천교 위를 지나는 차량들의 바퀴에 감긴 체인 소리가

only has to come along asking why things are so slow, and everyone speeds up in a flash."

Competition was impossible to avoid when they had so little power. Mi-jeong's considerable power was protecting the painting-room from competition. Cheol-sun finally understood why her team members had such a hard time avoiding competition. It was all about power. She had failed to become the shield that could protect her team. Each team member was obliged to take individual responsibility for any lag in production.

"It's because you come across as softies. Why do section chiefs and managers meddle with the production line? Because they think you're weak as water."

"You're right."

"Let's all three of us disappear tomorrow."

Mi-jeong proposed suddenly.

"We need to see what happens if all three of us are out of the picture. You two, above all, have to assert yourselves in front of the administrators. That way, no one will be able to bother you."

"Do you think the company will just sit back and watch?"

Min-yeong looked as if she could not imagine

요란했다.

"저기다!"

민영이 소리치는 것과 동시에 두 마리의 갈매기가 다리 난간 밑에서 날아올랐다. 눈이 내리는 수면 위로 날아가는 갈매기의 비행은 낮고 느렸다. 날갯짓은 바쁘게 계속됐지만 추진력을 갖진 못했다. 창공 드높이 선회하며 나는 바다갈매기의 그것과는 달랐다. 또 한 마리의 갈매기가 뒤이어 날았다. 그 갈매기의 날갯짓은 더욱 형편없는 것이어서 차라리 바다오리의 그것에 가까웠다. 겨우 수면 위를 바둥치며 나는 갈매기를 다 자신이 발견했다고 말하지 않았다.

"이제 세 마리만 더 찾으면 되는 거야."

"왜, 두 마리지. 네가 세 마리 찾았잖아."

"마지막 건 아냐, 날 줄 모르는 게 어떻게 갈매기야."

민영은 단호하게 마지막 한 마리의 갈매기를 자신이 발견한 숫자에서 제외시켰다. 자신의 권리를 위해 싸울 줄 모르는 사람은 노동자가 아냐. 철순이 그렇게 말한 건 노조 결성 준비를 시작한 뒤였다.

셋이 주도한 잔업 특근 거부는 예상 이상의 파문을 일으켰다. 화공부와 페인팅실 전원이 잔업을 거부했고 그

such a thing.

"What if they don't?" Mi-jeong answered with another question.

"Look, you're not like us. You'll be taking your period day off, while we should work without a break."

"You idiots. Who's stopping you? Try standing up together and fighting for once! Then see whether they give in or not! If you don't look out for yourselves, no one is going to do it for you. Look at you, Cheol-sun, you're a good talker—how come you haven't got your period day off?"

"I didn't want to be the only one."

Min-yeong suddenly recalled the production manager's face. He had always been kind to her. When she first came into the factory, he was her team leader. The workers were proud of him because he was the only manager who had risen from the bottom. He never forgot it, and he used to stress that he understood and cared about what was happening in the factory better than anyone else. Min-yeong had no way of knowing that he was the one who, on the basis of that understanding, had suggested to the owner the more than loving idea that they should divide the production line. She didn't

다음날 특근은 성형과 제형 부서에서까지 출근 않은 사람이 나왔다. 월요일 출근했을 때 셋을 기다리고 있는 것은 사직서와 각서였다. 그들은 탈의장에 가기도 전에 사무실로 불려 올라갔다.

백지 세 장이 주어졌다. 민영과 철순에게는 사직서가, 미정에게는 각서가 요구되었다. 8년과 7년 그리고 3년 동안 '우리 회사'라고 생각하며 다녀온 그들에 대한 '우리 회사'의 요구였다. 셋은 그 한 장의 백지가 주는 의미를 무섭게 깨달았다.

민영은 7년 동안 정든 세광물산과 자신의 관계를 생각해보았다. 구석구석마다 자신의 숨결과 손때가 묻은 세광물산은 민영에게 우리 회사이기를 거부하고 있다. 내밀어진 사직서는 세광물산은 너 따위의 것일 수 없다고 비웃고 있다. 세광물산은 어디까지나 사장 김세호의 것일 뿐이라고 호통쳤다.

나는 무엇인가, 세광물산에서 나의 의미는 무엇인가. 세광물산에서의 나의 7년은 무엇인가.

사무실의 모든 것이 갑자기 낯설게 느껴졌다. 근면·자조·협동, 벽 높은 데서 내려다보는 사훈이 낯설었다. 액자에 담긴 '사원을 가족처럼 회사일을 내 일처럼' 사장의 친

want to bother him. And it had been his encouragement that had kept her in the factory every time she was determined to quit.

"How about we take a boat trip to Yeongjong Island and back tomorrow? Then the day after is Sunday, we can stay home and rest."

Mi-jeong was taking another step forward.

"There's sure to be overtime."

Min-yeong was reluctant.

"Hey, why are you worrying for the owner? Live in a way that suits your position. Isn't that what he's always saying?"

"Besides, there's not much time until shipment is due."

"Really, someone loyal to Segwang. You're so loyal."

Mi-jeong clicked her tongue, tut, tut.

"You just want to make perfect attendance. Knock it off!"

"I couldn't care less about attendance."

Min-yeong was blushing as she responded. Not once had she missed a day of work in all the seven years she had been with Segwang. Except once. It had been a day in the summer, a day of floods. Her house had been so full of water there was no way

필도 새로운 의미로 다가왔다. 사무실 직원의 얼굴도 낯설다. 창밖으로 보이는 공장 건물도 낯설다. 강민영, 너는 일당 4,080원짜리 고용인 이상의 그 무엇도 아니야. 그리고 이제 사장은 네가 필요없어졌어. 매일 구매하던 4,080원짜리 물건을 이제는 다른 곳에서 구입하겠다는 거야. 내가 앉혀졌던 자리에 다른 누군가 앉혀져서 도료를 만지게 될 거야. 7~8년 동안 흐려져 있던 것이 한순간에 명확해졌다. 결코 사장과 자신들은 같은 줄에 서 있을 수 없음을, 7~8년이 아니라 70년 80년을 다녀도 그들이 서야 할 줄은 노동자의 대열임을 뼈아프게 확인하였다.

그놈의 정 때문에, 를 되풀이하며 다닌 세광에서의 세월은 이날부터 바뀌지 않을 수 없었다. 이날의 배신과 분노를 통해 가슴속 깊이 각인된 것은 노동자라는 세 글자였다.

그들이 총무과 사무실에서 사표와 각서를 종용받고 있을 때 생산과장은 현장 노동자들을 식당에 모아놓고 특별교육을 실시하고 있었다. 그는 사무실을 나가기 전에 민영에게 말하였다. 이럴 줄 몰랐다. 배신감을 느낀다, 고 말하는 그의 얼굴에는 찬바람이 일었다.

민영은 그의 말과 표정을 고스란히 그 자신에게 되돌려

she could get to work. *We mustn't leave this kind of blemish*, the current production manager had said, as he corrected her attendance card.

"I know you do care. I've been with Segwang the longest. Their attendance record is a noose that snares people. Even though you want to quit, you think, well, it's a shame after three years, and don't; then, it's a shame with four year's perfect attendance, and you don't, until it makes you skip breakfast and spend two thousand *won* for a taxi to earn four thousand *won* a day. I had perfect attendance for four years in a row, as well. All I got was a silver spoon and chopsticks at the factory's anniversary celebration. With a scrap of paper!"

"Instead of that, suppose we go to work tomorrow, but then not work overtime?"

Cheol-sun suggested an alternative.

"And rest on Sunday!"

Mi-jeong agreed happily.

"The others will like the idea, but..."

"It's up to the individual to work overtime or not. That's what the law says."

Cheol-sun encouraged the hesitant Min-yeong.

"We'll have to give them a reason. What about a repeal of the division of the sections?"

주고 싶었다.

그날의 사건은 미정이 직접 사장에게 비는 것으로 일단락되었다. 미정은 모든 책임이 내게 있다, 내가 사표를 쓰고 나가겠다, 민영과 철순은 용서해달라 빌었다. 세광이 좋아서 빈 것은 아니었다. 달리 갈 곳 없어서도 아니었다. 억울했다. 나가려 할 때마다 그렇게 붙들더니 이렇게 쫓아낼 수 있는가. 이렇게 쫓겨날 수는 없었다. 그리고 민영과 철순에게 어떻게든 책임을 지고 싶었다.

셋은 각서를 썼다. 모두 세광에 입사해서 처음 쓰는 것이었다. 그러나 그것은 결코 사장에 대한 치욕스런 항복문서만은 아니었다. 미정과 민영, 철순에게는 우정의 서약서가 되었고 동료들에게는 신뢰를 담보해주는 보증서가 되었다.

"철순이 고것 참 앙큼하지. 아주 계획적으로 우릴 꼬시려고 그랬던 거야. 여기 왔을 때부터. 우린 그것도 모르고 감쪽같이 속지 않았냐."

"미정 언닌 속은 게 억울해? 나도 일기장 보기 전까진 몰랐어요."

"억울하다는 게 아니라, 지만 통밥을 굴리고 우리에겐 그렇게 시침을 딱 뗄 수가 있냐 이거야."

"Okay."

The three brushed themselves off and stood up. Mi-jeong walked along between the two other women, locking arms with them. The tide hadn't come in yet, and a few seagulls were hovering over the mudflats. Min-yeong playfully picked up a rock and threw it. Five gulls rose into the air. They were so filthy they looked more black than white as they rose and flapped their way over to the mudflat opposite.

"I wonder what they live on."

Min-yeong mumbled in a concerned tone.

"Rusty water."

"Chemical residues."

As the two replied, Min-yeong asked another question:

"Surely no fish can live in that Shit Sea? Maybe they survive on the leftovers the restaurants chuck out?"

"They'll use their leftovers to feed pigs. Seagulls live off dreams."

Mi-jeong laughed at her own words.

"Those seagulls probably have no idea there's an open sea out there if they follow the ebbing tide. They're just like us workers, who think we're

철순은 이날의 일을 미정과 민영의 현장 노동자들에 대한 영향력과 지도력을 확실하게 확인할 수 있는 계기였다고 적고 있었다. 그리고 현장 동료들의 단결 가능성을 높이 여기게 되었다고 덧붙여놓았다.

"아마 그때 노조 얘기가 나왔다면 언닌 제시까닥 사장한테 꼰질러 바쳤을 걸."

"야 임마, 너 날 뭘로 아는 거야. 너야말로 김 과장한테 단박 일러바쳤을 거다."

미정이 민영의 주머니에 든 손으로 그녀의 허릴 꼬집었다.

"고것 옆에 있으면 이렇게 꼬집어줄 텐데 말야."

"살아나고 싶어도 위원장님 무서워서 못 살아나겠네."

갈매기는 다시 보이지 않았다.

"너무 늦었지. 그냥 가자. 돌아오는 길에 마저 찾기로 하고."

"위원장님, 순옥이 부모님 정말 찾아오면 어떡하지."

"나도 걱정이다. 학생애들한테 영향이 클 텐데."

doomed to poverty and humiliation. To them, this Shit Sea is all the sea there is."

"Wow, Cheol-sun's talking like a poet!"

Their shared conspiracy seemed to be making them merry. The three laughed loudly. Passers-by were staring at them.

People called the mudflats that lay sprawled between complexes seven and eight the Shit Sea. At high tides, the water came up to the embankment. When the water vanished with the ebbing tide, the filthy black mudflats revealed their disgusting expanse. Piles of garbage that the factories had secretly discarded the previous night rose along the margins of the mudflats. The rotting stench from the mixture of wastewater, sewage, garbage, mingled with the salty tang, offended people's noses. Shit Sea was the perfect name for it, and yet the factory workers, having nowhere else to go, used the embankment as their recreation area.

"Let's play at spotting seagulls. Who can spy five new seagulls, not counting the ones that flew away just now?"

Min-yeong took up the wager Mi-jeong proposed.

"Right, and the loser pays for the noodles!"

3

노동악법 개정하여 노동 3권 쟁취하자, 정문에 내걸린 현수막이 선홍정밀 노조의 위력을 웅변했다.

작업장의 단조해머가 하강할 때마다 요란한 마찰음이 귓전을 때렸다. 샤딩기를 돌리던 조합원들이 미정과 민영에게 아는 체를 했다. 안전모에 기름 얼굴을 한 조합원들을 알아볼 수 없었지만 반갑게 인사했다.

"아이고, 바쁘신 몸들이 어떻게 누추한 이곳까지 납셨습니까. 급한 일이 있음 부르실 일이지."

노조사무실에 들어서자 선홍정밀의 홍 위원장이 자리에서 일어나며 농담을 던졌다.

"미인이 두 분이나 들어서니까 사무실이 환해지는데요."

난로 속에 갈탄을 집어넣고 있던 선홍정밀의 사무장도 너스레를 떨었다.

"단도직입적으로 말씀드릴게요. 위원장님, 부탁이 있어 찾아왔어요."

미정의 어투는 지극히 사무적이었다.

"무섭게 그러지 말고 일단 앉아서 몸이나 좀 녹여요."

Mi-jeong and Min-yeong looked for seagulls until Incheon Bridge came in sight, but there was not one to be seen. Traffic was speeding across Incheon Bridge, which crossed the mudflats to the west, where the open sea began.

"Cheol-sun paid for noodles that time; one of us will have to pay this time."

"It's so cold they must all have gone into hiding."

The air was filled with the sound of snow chains on tires as cars sped across the bridge.

"Over there!"

As Min-yeong cried out, two birds flew up from under the bridge. It was snowing, and the birds flew slowly, just above the water. They were flapping their wings frantically, but couldn't work up any speed. They were very different from seagulls circling high up in the sky. Then another seagull appeared, following behind them. Its flight was even weaker than the others. It looked more like a duck. Neither of them claimed to have seen that gull as it struggled along close to the water.

"Only three more to go."

"What do you mean? Two more. You saw that other one, didn't you?"

"It doesn't count. A seagull that can't fly can't be

검은 얼굴의 근육이 강인해 보이는 홍 위원장이다.

"들어주실 거예요. 안 들어주실 거예요?"

"우리가 언제 세광 얘기 안 들어준 거 있어요?"

"요번엔 좀 어려운 거예요."

비로소 홍 위원장은 정색을 하고 미정을 바라봤다. 위원장의 책상 위엔 노조와 회사의 단체교섭안이 나란히 펼쳐져 있었다.

"돈이 좀 필요해요."

"얼마나?"

"좀 많아요. 삼백만 원."

난로 속의 갈탄을 헤집고 있던 사무장이 동작을 멈추고 돌아봤다. 놀란 것은 선홍정밀의 위원장과 사무장보다 민영이었다. 취사기 수리할 비용이나 꿀 줄 알고 따라왔었다.

"떼어먹지 않을게요. 저하고 우리 사무장 전세방 내놨는데 다음주에 나갈 거예요."

타닥타닥, 갈탄 타는 소리가 유난히 크게 울렸다.

"저, 그래도 삼백짜리 전세 살아요. 우리 사무장은 이백뿐이 안 되지만."

"뭐하는데 그렇게 많이 한꺼번에 필요해요?"

"학생애들 등록금이 모레까지예요. 안 내면 제적시키겠

called a seagull."

Min-yeong resolutely struck out the latest seagull from her score. Someone incapable of fighting for her rights is no worker. Cheol-sun had said that soon after they started preparing to form a union.

The refusal of extra work and overtime that the three of them organized raised a bigger commotion than they had expected. The chemicals department and the entire painting staff refused to work overtime on the Saturday; the next day, there were people even in the molding and forms units who did not report for work. When the three came to work on Monday, they found letters of resignation and written pledges waiting for them. They were called up to the office even before they had a chance to reach the changing-room.

They were handed three sheets of paper. Min-yeong and Cheol-sun were instructed to write letters of resignation; Mi-jeong a written pledge. After the eight, seven, and three years the three women had been working for what they thought of as "our company," that was what "our company" demanded of them. They were forced to recognize the terrifying implications of those sheets of paper.

Min-yeong pondered over the relationship she had

답니다. 부식비도 다됐고, 오늘 아침엔 취사기마저 고장이 나버렸어요."

홍 위원장은 담배를 꺼내 물었다. 짧은 침묵이 흘렀다.

"커피 한잔씩 들래요?"

사무장이 나직이 물었다.

"아침도 못 먹었을 텐데 우유로 뽑아드리지."

홍 위원장은 담배 연기를 길게 내뱉었다. 자판기에 동전을 집어넣기 전에 사무장은 옆에 놓인 모금함에 먼저 동전을 집어넣었다. 라면 박스로 만든 커다란 모금함이었다. 세광노조를 위한 모금함. 조합원 동지, 잠깐. 당신의 커피 한 잔이 세광 형제들의 겨울을 따뜻하게 합니다. 한 잔 마실 때마다 세광 동지들에게도 한 잔을 권하는 형제애를. 쟁의부.

사무장은 한 잔을 꺼낼 때마다 빠뜨리지 않고 모금함에 동전을 넣었다.

"식기 전에 드세요."

사무장이 김이 오르는 종이컵을 날라왔다.

"안 먹어요. 조합원들은 굶고 있는데 우리만 이걸 마셔요?"

"이건 완전히 땡깡이구만."

forged with Segwang over the last seven years, how fond she had become of it. Now our company, which contained traces of Min-yeong's breath and the dirt from her hands in every corner, was rejecting her. The letter of resignation was mocking her, telling her that there was no place for her kind at Segwang. This company, the letter was shouting, belonged to its owner, Kim Se-ho, and to him alone.

So what am I? What is my significance in Segwang? What have the past seven years here at Segwang been all about?

Suddenly, everything about that office appeared completely unfamiliar. Even the familiar slogans along the walls—Diligence, Self-Reliance, Cooperation!—seemed unfamiliar. The framed calligraphy, written by the president himself, which read, "Employees like my own family; company concerns like my own concerns," carried new meaning for her now. The faces of the office staff looked unfamiliar. The factory buildings, visible outside the window, looked unfamiliar. Kang Min-yeong, you're nothing more than a position worth 4,080 *won* per day. The owner doesn't need you any longer. Now he's going to go somewhere else to buy the object he

홍 위원장이 안타까운 웃음을 지었다.

"그럼 우리가 선홍정밀 아니면 어디 가서 땡깡을 부려요. 왜 위원장님도 조합원들 시켜서 우리 끌어낼래요. 노동청처럼."

"어허, 또 운다 울어, 다 큰 처녀가. 누가 안 해준다 그랬어요. 왜 그래."

"울긴 누가 울어요. 이 따위로 우리가 울 줄 알아요."

그렇게 말하는 미정의 음성엔 눈물이 묻어났다.

"사무장, 그 함 속에 든 거 삼백 안돼?"

"지금 농담할 때가 아네요. 위원장님."

미정이 홍 위원장의 말을 가로막았다.

"사무장, 우리 통장에 조합비 얼마나 남았어?"

"삼백은 돼요. 그런데 우리 맘대로 쓸 순 없잖아요."

"점심시간 다됐으니까 상집 대의원 연석회의 소집하지 뭐. 사무장이 현장 한 바퀴 돌래?"

사무장은 땀복 상의를 걸치며 사무실을 나섰다.

"잘될 거예요. 걱정 말고 우유 드세요."

"오기 전에 부서원들 얘기 들어보고 오라고 그래."

이미 문밖으로 나간 사무장을 향해 홍 위원장이 소리를 질렀다. 얼마 있지 않아 땀복에 안전화를 신은 간부와 대

paid 4,080 *won* for each day. Someone else will sit in the seat you've been occupying and apply the pigments. Something that had been unclear for the last seven or eight years suddenly became clear. She understood with a stab of pain that the workers and the owner could never be equal in rank; even if they worked there for the next seventy, eighty years, not just seven or eight years, the only rank for them would still be the workers' rank.

"It's all because of that goddam attachment," she had kept repeating to herself whenever she felt like leaving the company during the seven years. These years she had spent working at Segwang inevitably took on a new aspect. Thanks to that day's betrayal and fury, the word *worker* was stamped deep within her in a completely new spelling.

While they were being asked for letters of resignation and a written pledge in the general affairs office, the production manager had gathered the employees in the canteen for a special lecture. Before he left his office, he had addressed Min-yeong, *I never expected this. I feel betrayed.* As he spoke, his face grew cold and hard.

Min-yeong was tempted to throw the words and the expression right back at him.

의원들이 조합 사무실에 들어섰다.

“아침식사도 못 했다며요?”

“사장새낀 여태도 꼼짝 안 해요?”

제각기 한마디씩 격려의 말을 던졌다.

“우리 부서 조합원들은 꿔주라고 그러던데.”

“우리 부서에선 조합비는 건드리지 말고 모금을 한 번 더 하는 게 어떠냐는 사람도 많아.”

회의가 시작되었다.

미정과 민영은 자리를 피해주는 것이 좋을 것 같아 조합원 한 명을 따라 식당으로 갔다. 식판을 받아들고 줄을 섰다. 돼지고기가 든 김치찌개가 김을 올렸다.

미정은 식욕이 일지 않았다. 김치조차 없는 라면 가닥을 빨고 있을 조합원들이 눈에 어른거렸다.

“먹어요. 잘될 것 같던데.”

민영은 두어 숟갈만 먹어야지 했는데 빈 뱃속은 숟가락질을 멈추게 하지 않았다. 바닥까지 다 긁어 먹고도 아쉬웠다.

“우리도 손님들 찾아오면 식사 대접 할 수 있는 날이 올까?”

미정은 대답 대신 자신의 식판에서 밥을 덜어 민영에게

The events of that day concluded with a direct appeal to the owner by Mi-jeong. She pleaded: *It's all my fault; I should resign and quit; pardon Min-yeong and Cheol-sun.* She didn't beg because she liked Segwang. Nor because she had nowhere else to go. She felt aggrieved. Each time she had tried to quit in the past, they had done their utmost to stop her, so would they kick her out like this now? They shouldn't. Besides, she wanted to take responsibility somehow for Min-yeong and Cheol-sun.

The three each wrote a pledge. It was the first time for all of them to write one since they started with the factory. But the pledge was not really just a shameful document of surrender to the owner. It became a covenant of friendship among the three women, and a surety of trust in the eyes of their fellow workers.

"Cheol-sun was pretty audacious. She'd planned to get us involved from the very beginning. From the day she joined the company, and we had no idea, so we let ourselves be taken in completely, right?"

"Do you feel being deceived? Do you resent that, Mi-jeong Eonni? Until I read her diary, I had no idea, either."

"It's not resentment; it's the question of how she

옮겨놓았다.

"난 속이 안 좋아."

미정은 물끄러미 민영의 밥 먹는 모습을 건너봤다.

"민영아, 나 오늘 너무 뻔뻔하지."

"옆에서 지켜보기가 낯 뜨겁더라."

"미안하다, 그런 말 하기에는 이미 너무 많이 미안한 사람들이잖아. 고맙다는 말로 할 수 있는 도움은 벌써 옛날에 다 받았고."

선홍정밀의 헌신적인 지원은 세광 노동자들이 노조를 결성하고 임금인상을 요구하며 파업에 들어갔을 때부터 계속되었다. 세광 노동자들이 가장 걱정하던 구사대가 덤벼든 것은 노조를 결성하고 파업농성을 시작한 지 사흘 만이었다. 관리직 사원과 일부 남성 노동자들로 구성된 구사대는 각목과 쇠파이프를 휘두르며 정문을 뛰어넘어 덤벼들었다. 미친 듯이 각목을 휘두르는 그들 앞에서 민영은 물론 미정조차도 어찌해야 할 바를 몰랐다.

구사대와 조합원들이 뒤엉킨 운동장은 순식간에 아수라장이 되었다. 며칠 전까지만 해도 거역할 수 없는 상사와 허물없던 동료들의 폭력 앞에 조합원들은 공포와 배신감으로 떨었다. 제대로 한번 싸워보지도 못한 채 본관으

could know the picture while pretending not to."

Cheol-sun had written in her diary that that day's incident had been an opportunity to confirm effectively the influence and leadership that Mi-jeong and Min-yeong exercised among the workers. She added that it gave her confidence in the workers' ability to unite.

"If she had said anything about a labor union in those days, you would probably have reported it to the owner straight away."

"What do you take me for? I bet you would have taken the first opportunity to tattle to Manager Kim yourself."

Mi-jeong, who had her hand buried inside her friend's pocket, pinched Min-yeong's waist.

"If she were here, I reckon she'd get pinched like this."

"Even if she wanted to come back to life, she wouldn't; you scare her, Chief."

Once again, no more seagulls could be seen.

"It's late. Let's just go. We can look for them on our way back."

"Chief, what happens if Sun-ok's parents really do come to collect her?"

"That worries me, too. It'll affect the students a lot."

로 밀려났다. 본관 3층까지 쫓겨 올라갔을 때는 벌써 다섯 명이 병원으로 실려간 다음이었다. 남은 사람들 중에서도 간부들은 성한 사람들이 없었다.

머리가 깨지고 다리를 저는 동료들을 보며 비로소 조합원들은 복도에 신나를 뿌렸다. 책상을 꺼내다 계단을 막고 방어조를 편성했다.

불을 지르겠다는 위협에 접근을 포기한 구사대는 돌멩이를 던져 3층 유리창을 모두 박살냈다. 농성자들의 수가 곱절은 많았지만 대부분이 여자들이었다. 씨팔년들로 시작하여 온갖 더러운 욕설을 퍼부으며 운동장을 설치고 다니는 구사대를 보며 많은 조합원들은 여전히 겁에 질려 있었다.

상황을 변화시킨 것은 선홍정밀이었다.

퇴근시간이 되면서 이웃 공장의 노동자들이 몰려왔다. 정문 앞에 모여든 노동자들은 노래와 구호를 외치며 세광 노동자들을 응원했다.

"인간답게 살자는데 구사대가 웬말이냐!"

"노조탄압 분쇄하고 세광노조 사수하자!"

회사 측도 뒤질세라 옥외 스피커로 유행가를 틀어댔다.

"토요일은 밤이 좋아, 이 밤은 영원한 것, 그리움이 이

3

"Down with evil labor laws! Up with workers' rights!" The banner over the front gate of Seonheung Precision Mechanics indicated clearly the power of the labor union:

Every time the forge hammer in the workshop fell, a deafening crash struck the ears. Those working at the machines nodded at Mi-jeong and Min-yeong in recognition. With their helmeted, greasy faces, they could not recognize any of the unionists, but returned their greetings gaily.

"Why, to what do we owe the honor of a visit to our humble abode by such busy persons? You should have asked us to come if there was something urgent."

As soon as they entered the office of the Seonheung labor union, Hong, the union president, stood and greeted them jokingly.

"Look how bright the office is now you two beauties have come in."

The union secretary, who had been adding more coal to the stove, joined in the joke.

"We'll get right to the point. We have a favor to ask."

네. 어둠이 가고 낙엽이 지면 우리들은 헤매지만—"

치직거리는 스피커 소리가 공단을 뒤덮었다.

"노조탄압 자행하는 구사대를 씨 말리자!"

지원 온 노동자들은 한목소리로 외쳤다.

"쓸쓸한 갈대숲을 지나, 언제나 나를 언제나 나를 기다리는 너의 아파트—"

"강제와 감시 속에 우울하고 고통에 찬 죽음의 고역 같은 노동에서 해방되어—"

밤 이슥하도록 노동자들의 구호와 회사 측의 스피커 소리, 노동가와 유행가가 뒤섞이며 7공단을 떠들썩하게 했다.

끝까지 남았던 선홍정밀의 홍 위원장과 사무장 등이 구사대에 납치되어 얻어맞은 것은 이날 자정 가까이 돼서였다. 대부분의 사람들이 돌아간 다음 정문 앞에서 모닥불을 지피고 있던 홍 위원장 등을 구사대는 회사 안으로 끌고 들어갔다. 수십 명에게 둘러싸인 채 흠씬하게 두들겨 맞고 홍 위원장이 회사 밖으로 내팽개쳐졌을 땐 새벽녘이었다.

선홍정밀의 조합원들이 잔업을 제끼고 달려온 것은 바로 그날 저녁이었다.

쇠파이프로 무장한 선홍정밀의 조합원들은 세광을 향

Mi-jeong's tone was extremely businesslike.

"Hey, don't try to scare us. Why don't you sit down and thaw out first?"

President Hong's muscular face looked tough.

"Will you agree or not?"

"Have we ever not agreed to any requests from Segwang?"

"This time it's something a bit tricky."

President Hong at last turned serious and stared at Mi-jeong. The collective bargaining proposals prepared by the labor union and the company respectively lay open side-by-side on his desk.

"We need money."

"How much?"

"Rather a lot. Three million *won*."

The union secretary, still adding coal to the stove, froze for a moment and turned to look at them. Min-yeong was more surprised than either of the men. She thought they had come to ask for enough to fix the cooker.

"We'll not bilk the money. Both our union secretary and I have moved out of our rooms, so we'll get our key-money back some time next week."

The crackling of the coal burning in the stove sounded louder than usual.

해 공단가도를 내달렸다. 작업복 차림에 머리띠를 질끈 동여맨 젊은 조합원들이 앞장을 서고, 머리 희끗한 고참 노동자가 뒤따랐다. 아줌마 조합원들도 처지지 않고 숨을 몰아쉬며 함께 달렸다. 팔뚝을 걷어붙인 그들은 '정의사회 구현'의 공단 파출소와 '화해와 대화로 산업평화'의 수출공단 본부를 단숨에 지나쳐 달렸다.

"노동자로 태어나서 할 일도 많다만 너와 나 노조 지키는 영광에 살았다."

여기가 세광이야, 밀어붙여. 선홍정밀의 조합원들은 용접해버린 정문을 단번에 밀어제꼈다.

"어떤 새끼가 우리 위원장 깐 거야. 나와!"

죽여버려. 성난 파도처럼 밀려드는 선홍정밀 조합원들 앞에서 구사대는 하나둘 꼬리를 뺐다. 옆사람의 눈치를 흘끔흘끔 살피던 구사대는 생산과장이 뒷담을 넘는 것을 신호로 앞다투어 줄행랑을 쳤다.

미처 도망하지 못하고 현장 사무실에 남아 있던 부사장을 비롯한 상위 관리자들이 선홍정밀 쟁의부원들에게 끌려나왔다. 그토록 거만하던 부사장은 얼굴이 파랗게 질려 연신 고개를 주억거렸다.

"여러분, 이러시면 안 됩니다. 이성적으로 대화를 통해

"My room has a three million *won* deposit, you know. Though our secretary's room is only two million."

"Why do you need such a large sum all at once?"

"Our students have to pay their tuition fees by the day after tomorrow. Otherwise the schools say they'll be expelled. We've used all the money we have for food. And the kitchen stove broke down this morning."

President Hong lit a cigarette. A short silence followed.

"Would you like coffee?"

The secretary asked in a low voice.

"Make that milk. I'll bet they haven't eaten anything this morning."

Hong blew out a long stream of cigarette smoke. Before he slipped a coin into the dispenser, the secretary placed a coin into the collection box placed beside it. It was a large one made from an instant noodles box. On the outside, it read: *Collection for Segwang Union. Comrades, consider this: A cup of coffee for you can warm your comrades at Segwang this winter. Donate a cup to the comrades at Segwang whenever you drink a cup. Dispute Committee.*

서……"

안 되긴 뭐가 안 돼, 새꺄. 빗발치는 조합원들의 야유가 부사장의 말문을 막았다.

"이러시면 서로에게 불행한 일이 생깁니다……"

저 새끼 아직 정신 못 차렸군, 죽으려고 환장한 새끼 아냐. 조합원들의 야유에 다시 말을 이으려던 부사장은 입을 완전히 다물었다. 선홍정밀 노동자들의 고함 소리를 헤치고 오른팔에 붕대를 두른 홍 위원장이 앞으로 나섰다.

"여러분, 조합원 여러분. 이 사람들을 어떻게 할까요?"

한 손으로 들고 선 핸드마이크를 쟁의부장이 옆에서 받쳐들었다.

무·릎·꿇·려, 무·릎·꿇·려, 선홍정밀 조합원들은 한목소리로 외쳤다.

홍 위원장은 말을 끊고 부사장 일행을 돌아보았다. 당신들이 어떻게 해야 하는지 알겠지. 한 명 한 명 뚫어지게 쳐다본 다음 그는 조합원들을 향해 다시 말을 이었다.

"조합원 동지 여러분. 저의 팔 조금 다친 것, 사무장이 좀 얻어맞은 게 대단한 일은 아닙니다. 우리는 그 분풀이를 하러 온 것은 아닙니다. 우리 노동자들이 억눌리고 짓밟히며 살아온 것이 하루이틀이었습니까. 중요한 것은 우

The secretary never failed to drop a coin into the collection box every time he had a cup of coffee.

"Go ahead, drink it before it gets cold."

He came back bringing two steaming paper cups.

"Thanks, but no thanks. How could we drink this, when our comrades are starving?"

"You're really stubborn."

Hong smiled sympathetically.

"Where can we go and act this stubborn, if not to Seonheung? Why don't you have your union members throw us out, like the Labor Office did?"

"There you go, crying again. You're grown women now. Who's said we wouldn't help, anyway?"

"Crying? Who's crying? Do you think we'd cry over this kind of thing?"

Mi-jeong's voice was tearful as she spoke.

"Mr. Secretary, do you think there might be three million in that box?"

"This is no time for jokes, you know," Mi-jeong retorted curtly.

"Mr. Secretary, how much did we have left in our labor union account?"

"About three million. But we can't draw out that money whenever we want, can we?"

"It's lunchtime. Let's get all the representatives

리 공장뿐만 아니라 이 7공단 모든 공장에 민주노조를 튼튼히 세우고 모든 노동자들이 떳떳하게 요구하며 당당하게 주장하는 것입니다. 저기 세광의 나이 어린 여성 동지들을 보십시오."

홍 위원장은 붕대를 감은 손을 구부정하게 들어 본관의 현관 앞을 가리켰다. 어느새 달려나온 세광 조합원들이 이쪽을 지켜보고 있었다.

"일당 삼천칠백이십 원을 받으며 하루 열 시간 이상의 노동에 시달리는 저들의 일당 천오백 원 인상 요구가 지나친 요구입니까?"

껌값 주는 거야, 완전히 날강도들이구만. 선홍정밀 조합원들 사이에서 비난이 터져나왔다.

"아니면 그래도 배워보겠다고 밤에는 야간학교에 다니는 저 어린 동지들의 강제 잔업 철폐 요구가 각목과 쇠파이프로 찜질을 당해야 할 만큼 그토록 부당한 요구입니까? 먼저, 그래도 좌절하지 않고 열심히 살아왔고 또 살아가기 위해 몸부림치며 싸우고 있는 저 동지들에게 뜨거운 격려의 박수를 보냅시다."

열화와 같은 박수 소리가 터져나왔다.

"조합원 여러분. 세광의 어린 여성 노동자들이 구사대

together. Mr. Secretary, will you do the rounds?"

The secretary pulled on a sweatshirt as he left the office.

"It'll be OK, don't worry, just drink your milk."

"Tell them to listen to what the members of their departments have to say before they come here!"

Hong shouted after the union secretary who had already gone out of the door. Soon, the room began to fill with union leaders and representatives, all dressed in sweatshirts and safety shoes.

"I heard neither of you had any breakfast?"

"Has that bastard of an owner still not budged an inch?"

Each one uttered a word of support.

"The people in my section said to give you the money."

"Lots of folk in our department wonder if it wouldn't be better to hold one more fundraiser rather than touch the union funds."

The meeting began.

Mi-jeong and Min-yeong felt that it would be better if they weren't present, so they followed one of the union representatives to the canteen. They each took a tray and got in line. Steam was rising from the kimchi stew with pork.

와 악덕 기업주에 맞서 승리를 쟁취할 수 있도록 아낌없는 지원을 약속할 수 있겠습니까?"

"예."

"대답이 작습니다. 약속할 수 있겠습니까?"

"예!"

우렁찬 함성이 세광물산을 메아리쳤다.

"좋습니다. 우리는 오늘 바로 이 자리에서 세광물산 노동자들을 끝까지 지원하기로 약속했습니다."

선홍정밀의 홍 위원장은 성난 사자를 다루는 노련한 조련사와 같이 조합원들을 휘어잡으며 분위기를 이끌어갔다.

"그렇다면 오늘 우리들이 이 자리에서 해야 될 것은 딱 두 가지입니다. 첫째."

홍 위원장은 검지손가락을 세워 왼팔을 위로 내뻗었다.

"어제 있은 세광 조합원들과 지원 온 우리 노동자들에게 저질러진 구사대 폭력에 대한 공개 사죄와 보상 그리고 구사대의 즉각 해체입니다. 둘째."

홍 위원장은 다시 검지와 중지 손가락을 세운 팔을 흔들어 보였다.

"세광노조를 인정하고 평화로운 파업농성 투쟁을 보장

Mi-jeong had no appetite. All she could think about were the others back in the factory, snacking on instant noodles without so much as kimchi for flavor.

"Eat up. It looks like things will be OK."

Min-yeong had planned to eat only a couple of spoonfuls, but she was so hungry that she simply could not stop. She ate it all, down to the last drop, and still wished for more.

"Will there ever come a day when we'll be able to treat our guests to a warm meal?"

Instead of responding, Mi-jeong scooped the rice off her own tray and transferred it to Min-yeong's.

"My stomach's upset."

Mi-jeong watched Min-yeong eat it.

"Min-yeong, I've been really shameless today, haven't I?"

"I was too embarrassed even to look at you."

"Say I feel sorry? I reckon we owe them too much already to say that. And as for saying thank you, well, we received the kind of help it's right to say thank-you for a long way back."

Seonheung's generous support had been constant, ever since the Segwang employees first formed a labor union and went on strike demanding higher

하며 교섭에 성실히 임해야 한다는 것입니다. 만약 이것이 관철되지 않을 때는, 우리는 이 자리에서 한 발짝도 물러서지 않을 것입니다."

"우리 위원장 확실하다."

다시 고함 소리가 터져나왔다.

사·과·해, 사·과·해, 무·릎·꿇·고, 사·과·해. 두 차례의 파업투쟁으로 단련된 노동자들답게 선홍 조합원들과 위원장은 박자가 척척 맞았다. 보·장·해, 보·장·해, 노·조·활·동·보·장·해. 세광 노동자들도 목소리를 가다듬어 외쳤다.

선홍정밀 노동자들은 뒤늦게 달려온 사장으로부터 세광노조가 세 가지 사항에 대한 합의서를 받아내는 것을 보고 나서야 철수했다.

합의사항 (1) 구사대 폭력에 대한 공개 서면 사과 및 부상자 치료비 부담 (2) 구사대 해체 및 평화농성 보장 (3) 노조 인정 및 성실 교섭. 공장을 완전히 세광노조가 접수하는 것을 확인하고 난 뒤에야 비로소 선홍정밀 노동자들은 소리 높여 노래를 부르며 해산을 했다. 야간규찰 지원조로 연마 1반 20명의 조합원들을 남겨놓고.

이날부터 두 노조원들은 세광과 선홍정밀 노조를 피로

wages. The thing that the union members had dreaded most, the attack by the *kusadae* (save-our-company forces), had come three days after they formed the union and occupied the factory. The *kusadae*, a band consisting of clerks from the administration offices and ordinary male workers, came climbing over the front gate wielding square wooden clubs and metal pipes. Not just Min-yeong but even Mi-jeong were completely at a loss.

In moments, the sports-ground, where *kusadae* members and unionists had come to blows, was a scene of pandemonium. Seeing the violence of their superiors whom they had never thought of disobeying until a few days before and friendly comrades, the unionists stood shaking with terror and feelings of betrayal. Without putting up any kind of real fight, they retreated to the main building. By the time they had been driven up to the third floor, five of them had already been taken off to hospital. Among the rest, not one of the leaders had escaped injury.

Seeing their comrades, some with cracked skulls, some limping along, the union members poured paint thinner along the corridor. They dragged out desks to block the stairs and set up barriers.

맺은 연대노조라 불렀다.

어느새 굵어진 눈발은 하늘을 가득 채웠다. 선홍정밀의 운동장도 하얗게 뒤덮였다. 미정과 민영은 식당 창밖을 멍하니 지켜보고 앉아 있었다.

회의가 손쉽지 않은 모양이다. 식사시간이 끝난 지 벌써 30분을 넘기고 있었다.

“위원장님 방 빼고 나면 어디서 살 거야?”

“기숙사에 들어오면 되잖아.”

“만약 싸움에 지면?”

감옥에 가는 거지, 하는 말을 미정은 하마터면 입밖으로 내뱉을 뻔했다.

“지긴 왜 지니, 임마.”

“동생은?”

“동생도 지네 회사 기숙사에 들어가기로 했어.”

전세방을 빼겠다고 했을 때 동생은 의외로 담담했다.

—언니, 이젠 아주 미쳤군. 최저생계비가 어떻고 인간다운 삶이 어떻고 하더니 하나 있는 전세방마저 까먹는 거야? 나야 뭐라고 할말 있어? 10년 공장 생활 해서 번 건 언닌데.

미정이 벌어서 고등학교를 졸업시킨 동생이었다.

When they threatened to set the building on fire, the *kusadae* stopped their advance. Instead they stood outside the building and threw rocks at the third floor, shattering all the windows. The union members were twice the number of their attackers, but they were mostly women. They were gripped with fear at the sight of the *kusadae* storming over the sports-ground, hurling curses and every kind of obscenity.

It was Seonheung Precision Mechanics that had made all the difference.

At the end of work, workers from neighboring factories came flocking. They stood at the front gates chanting songs and slogans to cheer on the Segwang workers.

"We only want to live as human beings, who needs *kusadae*?"

"Down with the oppression of unions—defend the Segwang labor union!"

Not to be outdone, the company sent popular songs blaring from speakers mounted on the roof of the factory.

On Saturdays, I love the night, a night that never ends, a certain yearning surges in me. I wander around when darkness fades and autumn leaves

—너도 기숙사에 들어가서 좀 지내. 싸움 끝나면 다시 같이 살도록 해. 그리고 내게 혹시 무슨 일이 있더라도 절대 놀라지 말고. 언니가 남에게 해서 안 될 일을 한 적은 없지 않니.

"위원장님, 만약 싸움에 지면 내 방에서 같이 살아요."

"질 일 없다고 그랬잖아."

"만약."

"만약도 없다니까."

민영은 뾰로통해져서 창밖으로 눈길을 돌렸다.

"위원장님, 사무실에 가보세요. 잘됐어요."

"식사는 했어요?"

회의를 끝낸 조합의 간부와 대의원들이 왁자지껄 떠들며 식당에 들어섰다.

"오늘은 또 무슨 음모 꾸미느라고들 이렇게 늦었어?"

식당 아줌마들이 간부들에게 친근감을 표시했다.

"아줌마들 월급 올리자는 얘기하다 늦었으니까, 고기 좀 많이 줘요."

"으이구, 맨날 우리 땜이라지. 위원장님은 왜 안 와?"

"곧 올 거예요."

대의원들에게 고개를 숙여 보이고 조합 사무실로 향했

fall, but...

The sound from the fizzling speakers spread across the whole complex.

"Exterminate the *kusadae* who help oppress labor unions!"

The workers who had come to support the strikers shouted back.

...Past the lonely reed bed, your apartment is always waiting, always waiting for me...

"Liberation from the deadly drudgery of work, grim and full of pain amidst constraint and compulsion!"

The workers' slogans and the company's speakers, worker's songs and popular tunes, echoed loudly across complex seven deep into the night.

It was almost midnight when President Hong, the union secretary and some others from Seonheung were captured and beaten up by the *kusadae.* Most people had gone home, Hong and a few others were stoking a bonfire at the front gate when some of the *kusadae* gang had come and dragged them inside the factory. It was dawn when Hong was thrown out of the factory, after having been beaten up, surrounded by a crowd of men.

다. 사무장이 차트병 출신답게 공고문을 가지런히 적어내려가고 있었다.

임시 상집 대의원 연석회의 결과보고. 하나, 조합비 중 삼백만 원을 세광노조에 대출한다. 둘, 만약 위 금액이 3개월 이내에 회수가 불가능할 때는 상집 대의원의 월급에서 일괄 공제한다. 셋, 월급봉투 잔돈 모으기와 자판기 모금액(합계 423,100원)은 전액 전기장판을 구입하여 세광노조에 전달한다.

홍 위원장은 책상 모퉁이에 걸터앉아 문구를 불렀다.

“줄 바꿔서 넷, 콤마 하고 세광노조의 야간규찰 지원에 해당된 부서는 대의원의 책임하에 한 사람도 빠짐없이 참여한다. 마침표 하고 끝. 줄 바꿔서 전진하는 선봉노조 선홍정밀 노동조합.”

“월급봉투 잔돈 모으기가 뭔가 아세요?”

매직펜 뚜껑을 닫은 사무장이 장난스럽게 물었다.

“월급봉투에서 지폐를 꺼내고 잔돈은 모조리 쏟아붓는 거예요. 월급날 총무과 앞에서 저는 바께쓰를 들고 있고 위원장님이 선동을 하죠. 자, 동전은 있는 대로 모두모두 쏟아부으세요. 있어도 그만 없어도 그만인 동전은 모두 다 털어요.”

That evening, the workers from Seonheung refused to do overtime and came racing over.

Armed with steel pipes, the union members from Seonheung ran down the road toward Segwang. The younger union members led the way, wearing their working clothes, with sashes tied tightly round their heads. Veteran workers, their hair streaked with gray, followed behind. Middle-aged women workers didn't lag behind, either. They took a deep breath and went running. Sleeves rolled up, they ran without pausing past the police station, where a sign read "Build a More Just Society," and the export headquarters office with its sign "Peace in the workplace through reconciliation and negotiation!"

"We were born as workers, so we have plenty to do, but it is an honor for you and me to protect the union."

"Here's Segwang, heave-ho!" The Seonheung unionists toppled the main gate that had been welded shut with a single push.

"Who's the bastard that beat up our leader? Out with him!"

"Kill them all!" Faced with the furious Seonheung union members, the *kusadae* gang, one by one,

사무장은 시장 바닥의 장사치마냥 손바닥까지 탁탁 치며 위원장의 선동 모습을 익살스럽게 흉내냈다.

"사무장 저거 사기치네. 바께쓰 들고 있었던 게 나지 임마. 선동하는 게 좀 쪽팔렸던 모양이지, 왜. 얼굴이 좀 새빨개져서 그렇지 잘하던데."

"막연히 모금하면 부담스럽잖아요. 작게 내면 찜찜하고. 지폐는 안 받고 동전만 받는다 딱 하니까 그런 거 없잖아요."

"그래도 다 모으니까 바께쓰가 묵직하더라구요."

"위원장님, 사무장님……"

미정은 무슨 말인가를 해야 했다.

"잊지 않을게요."

미정은 그 이상 다른 말을 할 수 없었다.

"힘냅시다."

홍 위원장은 오른손 주먹을 굳게 쥐어 보였다.

"꼭 이겨야 합니다."

사무장이 덧붙였다.

started retreating. They kept a careful eye on one another and when the production manager jumped over the back wall, they took that as a sign, quit the fight and took to their heels.

Some officers, who had been in the office and were not able to escape, including the vice-president of the company and some high-ranking managers, were dragged out by the team from Seonheung. The previously arrogant vice-president's face was dark with fear as he kept bowing.

"Gentlemen! This isn't right. Can't we talk like reasonable human beings..."

Not right? What's not right? Bastard! A shower of catcalls from the unionists silenced the vice-president.

"If it goes on like this, we'll all end up regretting it ..."

That idiot still hasn't got it. Has the bastard gone nuts and want to get himself killed? At last the unionists' mockery reduced the vice-president, still intent on speaking, to silence. Hong then made his way through the shouting crowd of workers, his right arm wrapped in a bandage.

"Members, union members! What shall we do with these people?"

4

해를 넘겼다. 추석과 성탄절, 새해 아침까지 농성장에서 둥우리를 틀고 보냈다.

초저녁부터 불이 켜진 3층 중앙의 사무실은 자정이 넘도록 불이 꺼지지 않았다.

상집회의는 침울했다. 미정이 이날처럼 화를 낸 적은 없었다.

"말을 해, 입이 있으면 말을 해보란 말야! 누가 그 따위 짓을 시켰어?"

모두들 고개를 숙인 채 굳게 입을 다물고 있다.

"순옥이 너, 대답해. 누가 그 따위로 돈 벌어오라고 그랬어?"

순옥은 입술을 깨물고 눈을 똑바로 뜨고 있다.

"도대체 니들이 몇 살이야? 니들은 학생이야, 학생."

어제 저녁 미정은 처음으로 전철역엘 갔다. 조합원들이 전철역에 커피 장사를 시작한 지 열흘 만이었다. 어젯밤은 유난히 바람이 세차게 불어와 장사를 나가지 말라고 제지했지만 순옥은 기어코 조합원들을 데리고 나갔다.

조합원들을 내보내고 상집회의를 하는 동안 바람은 쉬

He was holding a microphone with one hand and the head of the negotiating team was supporting it.

On Their Knees! On Their Knees! The crowd of unionists chanted as one.

Hong stopped speaking and turned to look at the vice-president and the others with him. *You know what you need to do now, don't you?* He stared intently at each one of them before turning back to the unionists.

"Comrades! The fact that my arm is a bit hurt, or that our secretary has got beaten up, is not important. We're not here to retaliate for that. We workers have spent our whole lives being oppressed and trampled on. The important thing is to firmly establish democratic unions in every factory of industrial complex seven, not just our factory alone, so that all the workers can stand up to demand and claim what they deserve. Just look at our young women comrades of Segwang!"

Hong raised his bandaged hand and pointed awkwardly at the porch of the factory's main building. The Segwang union members had come running out and were looking in their direction.

"Is it really excessive to demand that those women, who are earning 3,720 *won* for more than ten hour's

지 않고 몰려와 창문을 뒤흔들었다. 미정의 머릿속엔 장사 나간 조합원들의 얼굴만 떠올랐다. 미정은 서둘러 상집회의를 끝내고 전철역으로 나갔다. 가까이 다가가지 않고 멀찌감치 서서 조합원들이 장사하는 모습을 지켜봤다. 하행 전철이 멈춰서자 사람들이 몰려나왔다. 열 명이 넘는 조합원들은 재빨리 그들 중에서 한 명씩을 붙들고 매달렸다.

"따뜻한 커피 마시고 가세요. 이백 원이에요."

"위장 폐업 분쇄 커피예요. 도와주세요."

뿌리치고 가는 사람도 있고 영문도 모르고 끌려와서 커피를 마시는 사람들도 있었다. 근심스런 얼굴로 조합원들의 등을 두드려주며 지폐를 놓고 가는 사람도 어쩌다 눈에 띄었다. 그러나 그것은 어쩌다였다.

다시 한 대의 전철이 도착했다.

조합원들은 필사적으로 매달렸다. 사람들은 붙잡히지 않으려고 계단을 뛰어올라갔다. 미정은 가슴이 미어졌다. 그녀는 조합원들이 이렇게 커피를 팔아 오는 줄 몰랐다. 하루 저녁에 5~6만 원씩 팔아 오는 조합원들을 대견스럽게 여기며 그저 고생했다고 격려해온 자신이 죽이고 싶도록 미웠다.

work a day, should receive a raise of 1,500 *won* a day?"

Why, that's the price of a pack of gum. It's sheer daylight robbery. Critical comments fused among the Seonheung unionists.

"Or is it so wrong of those young workers to ask to be dispensed from compulsory overtime simply because they want to study at night school, is it so wrong that they deserve to be knocked about with wooden clubs and steel pipes? First of all, let's give a big hand in support of our comrades who are refusing to be discouraged, who have done all they could until now and are struggling with all their might to live well in the future, too!"

The crowd exploded in waves of wild applause.

"Union members! Can we pledge our unbounded support in helping these young women unionists of Segwang gain a clear victory over the *kusadae* and the evil factory owner?"

"Yes!"

"You're not loud enough! Can we pledge that?"

"YES!"

Their resonant shouts echoed off the walls of the Segwang factory.

"Right. Today, on this spot, we have pledged to

순옥은 손님을 데리고 와 옆에서 얼쩡거리는 조합원들을 독려했다.

미정은 장사가 끝날 때까지 그 아픈 광경을 지켜보고 있었다.

축 늘어진 어깨를 한 조합원들은 버스도 타지 않고 다섯 정거장을 걸어서 세광으로 돌아왔다. 그들의 힘없는 발걸음에서는 좀 전의 커피를 팔 때 보이던 뻔뻔스러움과 집요함을 찾아볼 수 없었다. 미정은 그들의 뒤를 따라 공장으로 돌아왔다.

"지금까지 계속 그런 식으로 사람들에게 커피를 판 거야?"

"처음엔 그렇지 않았어요. 조금씩 조금씩 많이 팔려고 하다보니 어제처럼 된 거예요. 그런데 그게 뭐 그렇게 잘못됐다는 거예요?"

순옥은 대들었다.

"야, 너 아직도 잘했다 이거야? 애들 그렇게 하는 것 보고도 아무렇지도 않았단 말야. 니들이 거리의 여자들이야? 애들을 창녀로 만들 작정이야?"

"위원장님은 우리가 장사하고 있는 게 그렇게 마음이 아팠어요? 아니면 자존심이 상했어요?"

support to the very end the workers at Segwang."

Hong led on the Seonheung workers, building up the suspense like an expert trainer controlling an angry lion.

"Today there are two things that have to be done here and now. First..."

Hong lifted the index finger as he held up his left arm.

"First, we want a public apology and compensation for the violence the *kusadae* team inflicted on the Segwang union members and our workers who were supporting them yesterday, and the immediate dissolution of the *kusadae*."

He again waved his arm, raising the index and middle fingers.

"Second, they must recognize the Segwang labor union, guarantee the right to peaceful strikes and sit-ins, and engage in sincere negotiations. If these are not achieved, we will not budge from this place!"

"You're a real leader!"

Shouts rose again.

A-po-lo-gize! A-po-lo-gize! Down-on-your-knees-and-apo-lo-gize! The Seonheung unionists and their leader were now clapping their hands in rhythm,

미정은 뚫어지게 순옥을 노려봤다.

학생들 등록금 낸 돈이 위원장과 사무장의 전세방 뺀 데서 나온 것이란 사실이 알려지자 순옥은 벌어서 갚아야 한다고 앞장서 주장했다. 미정도 반대하지 않았다. 지금까지 이웃 노조와 학생들, 민주단체에서 모금해온 돈을 앉아서 받기만 했다. 그러나 모금도 한두 달의 얘기였다. 스스로 벌겠다고 나서는 조합원들이 대견스러웠다.

"회사 쪽에서 그 광경을 봤으면 뭐라고 선전했겠어?"

"그게 그렇게 무섭고 중요해요?"

미정은 자리에서 일어나 창가로 갔다. 건너편 식당 건물 옥상에서 규찰을 맡은 조합원들이 모닥불을 피워놓고 노래를 부르고 있었다. 누가 저들에게 키보다 큰 쇠파이프를 들게 만들었는가. 불길에 일렁이는 그들의 모습을 미정은 묵묵히 지켜봤다. 누가 낯 모르는 사람들의 팔에 매달려 커피를 팔도록 만들었는가.

상집 간부들은 의자 깊숙이 몸을 묻은 채 가끔 창가에 등을 돌리고 선 미정을 돌아보았다. 잠바 깃을 세운 미정의 뒷모습이 고집스럽다.

"우린 뭐 그짓 하고 싶어서 하는 줄 알아요? 우리도 구걸하듯이 장사하기 싫어요. 우리도 현장에 들어가서 일하

workers disciplined by their two previous strikes. *Gua-ran-tee! Gua-ran-tee! Gua-ran-tee U-nion Activities!* The Segwang workers raised their voices and joined in.

The Seonheung workers withdrew only after they had seen the Segwang union receive a written agreement from the owner, who had arrived belatedly.

The agreement included: (1) a public apology for the violence of the *kusadae* and payment of medical costs for those wounded; (2) dissolution of the *kusadae* and a guaranteed right to peaceful strike; (3) recognition of the union and sincere negotiations. Once they were sure that the factory was fully controlled by the Segwang union, the Seonheung laborers dispersed. Twenty Grinding Section 1 union members stayed behind as a supporting night guard force.

From that day on, the members of the two unions called unions of the Segwang and Seonheung Precision Mechanics a union united by a blood bond.

The snowflakes had thickened until they were filling the sky. The sports-ground of the Seonheung Precision Mechanics factory was completely white.

고 싶어요. 신나 냄새도 그리워요. 학교에서 다른 회사 취직한 애들이 월급봉투 타오는 것 보면 얼마나 부러운지 아세요?" 맺힌 것 많은 순옥이었다.

순옥과 조합의 설득 편지에도 불구하고 순옥의 아버지는 공장을 찾아왔다.

"머리에 피도 안 마른 것이 뭘 안다고 데모질이야, 데모질이."

머리가 하얗게 센 순옥의 아버지는 대뜸 딸의 뺨부터 후려쳤다.

"아빠, 그게 아녜요."

"아니긴 뭐가 아냐. 저 벽에 시뻘겋게 휘갈겨 써놓은 게 빨갱이가 하는 짓이 아니고 뭐야. 당장 짐 싸들고 오지 못해!"

"우린 나쁜 짓을 하고 있는 게 아녜요. 전 죽어도 여기서 나가지 않을 거예요."

"뭐가 어쩌고 어째."

아버지는 순옥의 머리채를 휘어잡았다. 미정이 옆에서 말렸지만 소용이 없었다. 조합원들은 2층 기숙사에서 처음부터 내려다보고 있었다. 참혹한 광경이었다.

"그런 식으로 하려면 김세호한테 머리 숙이고 들어가는

Mi-jeong and Min-yeong sat staring silently through the canteen windows.

It looked as though things were not going smoothly in the meeting. Already, thirty minutes had passed since the end of the lunch break.

"Where are you going to live if you give up your room?"

"I can move into the dorm."

"What if we lose the struggle?"

Then I'll be in jail, Mi-jeong almost said but stopped herself at the last moment.

"Lose? Why should we lose?"

"What about your sister?"

"She's decided to move into the dorm in her factory."

Her sister had taken the news about moving out surprisingly calmly: *You're really crazy. Talk about minimum living expenses, about living human lives, and now it's costing you your one and only room? What do you expect me to say? You're the one who earned the money working in a factory for the past ten years.*

Mi-jeong had supported her sister through high school. *Go and live in the dorm for a while. We'll live together again once the struggle's over. And*

게 나아."

미정의 목소리가 올라갔다. 순옥이 자리에서 발딱 일어섰다.

"그런 식, 그런 식 하는데 그런 식이 뭐 어쨌다는 거예요. 먹고 살 돈이 있어야 싸우는 거 아네요. 다른 방법이 있음 얘길해보란 말예요. 돈 2억 받고 끝낼 거예요? 전 2억이 아니라 이백 억을 준다고 해도 철순 언닐 배신할 수 없어요."

"야 임마, 내가 언제 돈 받고 끝내자고 그랬어?"

사장은 노동청을 통해 협상을 제의해왔다. 농성조합원 65명에게 2억의 보상금을 주겠다고 했다. 그리고 조합원들의 정신적 피해에 대해서는 다시 중앙일간지 두 곳에 사과 광고를 싣겠다고 덧붙였다. 노동청은 조합원 전원의 타회사 취업을 책임지겠다고 제안했다.

간부들은 냉담했다.

"개자식, 그 돈으로 정상 가동하면 되잖아."

사장은 보상금의 액수가 더 올라갈 수 있음도 암시했다. 그러나 공장 가동만큼은 어떤 일이 있어도 못 한다는 거였다.

"사과 광고, 언제는 안 실었어?"

don't get upset if something should happen to me. You know I've never hurt anyone.

"If we lose, you can move in with me."

"We won't lose. I've told you so."

"Just in case."

"There's no in case."

Min-yeong was growing sulky, so she looked toward the window.

"You must go back to the office. It's all worked out alright."

"Have you eaten?"

The union leaders and representatives were coming into the canteen, chatting noisily.

"So what kind of conniving plot have you been cooking up that it kept you this late?"

The kitchen women showed their affection for the representatives.

"We've been discussing how to get a raise for you all. Give us lots of meat, will you?"

"Go on, blame it on us, as usual. Isn't the president coming?"

"He's on his way."

The two took their leave of the representatives and headed for the union office. The secretary was writing out a poster neatly, showing the clerical

"취업 보장 좋아하네. 세광 다닌 줄 알면 어떤 미친 사장이 받아주겠다."

그러나 조합원들 일부가 동요했다. 머릿속에서 2억 원이 65로 나눗셈되었다. 1인당 3백만 원이 넘는 돈이다. 순옥도 그 정도 산수는 했다. 한 달에 5만 원씩 붓던 적금이 3백만 원이 되려면 꼬박 5년을 부어야 한다는 것도 셈이 되었다.

"더러운 돈 받기보다 벌어서 싸우겠다는 일인데 뭐 잘못됐단 말예요!"

박차고 나가는 문소리가 그녀의 말끝을 맺었다.

순옥이 끝내 아버지에게 끌려가지 않을 수 있었던 건 통장 덕분이었다.

—아빠, 우리가 일 안 하는 게 아니란 말예요. 보세요. 내년에 아빠 환갑 해드리려고 매달 5만 원씩 적금 부어오던 것마저 사장 때문에 중단했어요. 노조 없애려고 사장이 문을 닫아버린 것이란 말예요.

"순옥이 커피 장사를 하는 방법이 지나치긴 했지만 위원장님이 그토록 화를 내는 것도 옳지는 않다고 봅니다. 우리가 더욱 중요하게 바라봐야 할 것은 조합원들 자신이 스스로의 힘으로 투쟁 자금을 확보하겠다는 의지입니다."

skills he had learned in the army.

Result of a Special Meeting of Union Representatives

One: Three million *won* from the sum in the union account is to be transferred to the Segwang union.

Two: If this amount cannot be repaid within three months, it will be deducted as a lump sum from the salaries of the representatives.

Three: Any loose change from monthly salary envelopes and the sum in the box by the coffee dispenser (total 423,000 *won*) will be used to purchase electric blankets for the Segwang union.

Hong was perched on one corner of the desk, dictating.

"New line—Four—colon—Attendance is required of all members of sections assigned for night-guard duty, with representatives held responsible—period—new line—Seonheung Labor Union at the Forefront and on the Move."

"Do you know how to collect loose change from the monthly salary?"

The secretary spoke jokingly as he replaced the

문화부장이 말문을 열었다.

"커피 판매 문제는 접어두고 사장이 제시한 협상안에 대해서 얘기를 해봅시다."

"그 얘기 이미 끝난 거 아녜요. 우리의 요구는 단 하나 정상 가동입니다. 더 무슨 얘기가 필요해요."

총무부장이 문화부장의 말을 가로막고 나섰다.

"우리가, 간부들이 싫다, 말도 안 된다고 해서 있는 것이 없는 것으로 되진 않아요. 실제로 조합원들은 술렁거리고 있어요. 조합원들의 생각을 먼저 파악해야지 우리만 생각해선 안 되는 겁니다."

"그래서 돈을 받자, 그 얘기예요? 간단히 얘기해요."

"아니, 말을 왜 자꾸 그 따위로 합니까. 내 얘긴 술렁거리는 조합원들을 결집시켜야 된다는 겁니다."

둘의 목소리가 올라갔다.

"위원장님이 말씀 좀 하세요."

민영이 다시 자리로 돌아온 미정에게 말을 권했다.

"이번에 사장이 내놓은 협상안으로 조합원들의 일부가 흔들리고 있는 것은 사실입니다. 그동안 우리는 너무 긴 싸움으로 지쳐 있고 사실 승리의 전망도 확실치 않습니다."

회사는 노조가 2억 원 협상안을 거부하자 조합원들에

cap on the felt pen.

"People take their salary envelopes, remove the bills, then pour out all the loose change. On payday, I stand in front of the office of general affairs with a bucket in one hand while our leader here urging people. *Come on, tip it out, every last penny of the loose change you've got. Tip out all the coins that will make no difference to you, whether you have them or not.*"

The secretary jokingly imitated the way Hong prodded the workers, even clapping his hands like a market-place salesman.

"He's having you on, that secretary of ours. I was the one standing with the bucket. He looked embarrassed having to harangue people. He blushed a bit, but he did a good job."

"Just asking for contributions without specifying the amount can make people uncomfortable, you know. People feel embarrassed if they only give a small sum. But only asking for coins and refusing banknotes avoids all that."

"And the bucket was really heavy after everyone dropped their coins."

"You know..."

Mi-jeong felt she had to say something.

대한 개별공작에 나섰다.

—지금 농성장에서 나오면 3백만 원을 준다. 이것이 마지막 기회다. 이 이후에는 1원 한 푼도 없다.

집으로 찾아가 가족들까지 유혹했다.

"상당한 현찰로 협상안을 낸 것은 우리 세광의 투쟁이 지역의 임투와 연결되는 것을 막으려는 노동청의 방침 때문인 것 같습니다. 어느 기자에게 들은 바에 따르면 경찰, 안기부, 노동청이 모인 관계기관대책회의에서도 세광투쟁을 가장 목의 가시로 여기고 있답니다. 그러나 저들의 이러한 협상 요구도 그동안 우리가 싸워온 투쟁의 성과들입니다. 저들의 이 작은 후퇴 앞에서 우리의 대열이 흐트러진다면 150일간에 걸친 우리의 투쟁은 물거품이 되고 말 것입니다."

"이렇게 하는 건 어떨까요?"

선전부장이 다른 사람들의 눈치를 살피며 조심스레 말문을 열었다.

"한 1억 더 따로 달래서 철순 언니 기념관 지으면. 실제로 정상 가동은 쉬운 일 같지 않고 더 끌다 나중에 하나씩 떨어져나가서 흐지부지되는 것보다 낫잖아요?"

"철순이가 원하는 건 기념관이 아녜요."

"We'll never forget."

Mi-jeong could say nothing more.

"Let's be strong."

Hong raised his right hand closed tightly in a fist.

"You must win."

The union secretary added.

4

The year ended. The Chuseok Harvest Festival, Christmas Day, New Year's Day, they spent them all installed in the occupied factory.

The lights were turned on in the main office on the third floor early one evening and were not turned off until well past midnight.

The meeting of the executive committee was a gloomy one. Mi-jeong had never been so angry.

"Start talking! If you have mouths, use them! Who told you to act like that?"

The group stood silent, heads bowed and mouths shut.

"Sun-ok, answer me. Who told you to earn money that way?"

Sun-ok was biting down hard on her lower lip and looking straight ahead.

총무부장이었다.

여러 의견들이 쏟아져나왔다. 결론은 쉽게 나지 않았다. 현실적으로 승산이 없는 만큼 돈을 받고 끝내자는 의견은 한두 명이 내세웠다. 나머지는 전원 구속이 되더라도 싸우자는 쪽이었다.

"이 문제는 상집에서 다수결로 정할 문제는 아닌 것 같습니다. 앞으로 일주일간 조합원들과 오늘 우리가 했던 회의 내용을 가지고 함께 토론해서 결론을 내리겠습니다. 각 조별로 통일된 의견을 구정 연휴가 끝나는 날 저녁까지 마련하도록 합시다."

상집 간부들은 한결같이 말없이 회의실을 빠져나갔다. 미정과 민영만이 남았다.

미정은 무너지듯 의자에 주저앉았다. 민영이 석유난로를 미정 옆으로 옮겼다.

"왜, 들어가 자지 않고."

미정은 팔짱을 끼고 의자에 기대 누운 채였다.

"위원장님도 같이 들어가죠."

민영은 난로 앞에 쪼그리고 앉아 손을 내밀었다. 난로는 제 몸뚱이 하나를 겨우 데웠다. 미정의 머릿속으로 지난 7개월의 세월이 필름처럼 지나갔다. 노조를 결성한 뒤

"How old do you think you are? You're only students, for goodness' sakes, students!"

The night before, Mi-jeong had gone to the subway station for the first time. It had been ten days since the union members had started selling coffee at the station. The wind was particularly cold that night and she had tried to talk them out of going, but Sun-ok had insisted they should go.

Once they had left, there had been a committee meeting, during which the wind had kept on blowing, rattling the windows. Mi-jeong could think of nothing but the union members out there selling coffee. She ended the meeting as soon as she could and walked to the subway station. She stood some distance away and watched them. As soon as an incoming train came to a stop, the passengers came pouring out. Each of the dozen or so unionists immediately grabbed one of the passengers and clutched hold of him.

"Have a hot cup of coffee. Only 200 *won*."

"It's coffee for a strike to stop them closing down our factory."

Some passengers shook them off, some let themselves be led without understanding what was going on and drank the coffee. A few people gave

단 하루도 평화는 없었다.

이제는 마지막 고비에 서 있다.

"요즘도 애들 밥해 먹이느라고 고생이지?"

"애들한테 미안하지 뭐. 김치 한 가지뿐이잖아. 국도 없이."

반찬 투정하는 조합원들은 없어졌다. 부식비가 별도로 책정되지도 않았다. 밥과 김치가 전부였다. 어쩌다 시장을 다녀와서 반찬을 내놓으면 되레 역정을 부렸다. 돈 없는데 뭐하러 이런 데 쓰느냐고. 해가 바뀌면서 조합원들은 강도 높은 투쟁이 다가오고 있음을 직감하고 있었다.

아무도 입밖에 내지 않았지만 감옥은 물론 그보다 더한 희생이 요구되고 있다는 것을 알고 있었다.

"미정 언니, 인간적으로 물어볼 게 있는데 솔직히 대답할 수 있어?"

미정은 고개를 끄덕였다.

"미정 언니, 감방에 갈 생각이지."

미정은 표정도 대답도 없었다.

"누구누구 감방에 갈 건데?"

희미한 노랫소리가 들렸다. 건너 건물 옥상에서 규찰조가 부르는 노래다. 벽시계는 새벽 2시 20분을 넘고 있었

the girls a look of commiseration, a banknote, and a pat on the back. But they were few and far between.

Another train pulled in.

Again the girls clung desperately to passengers. Many darted up the stairs, trying to avoid being snared. For Mi-jeong it was heartbreaking. She had not dreamed that the strikers were selling coffee this way. She had been so proud of these girls, earning 50 or 60,000 *won* every evening, and had kept encouraging them on their return. Now she detested herself for what she had foolishly been doing.

Sun-ok kept bringing customers over for coffee, encouraging the other union members who were prowling around.

Mi-jeong stayed where she was and watched these painful scenes until the very end.

The girls, shoulders drooping, walked the five bus stops back to the factory rather than ride a bus. There was no sign in their weary footsteps of the impudence and persistence they had displayed previously, while they were selling the coffee. Mi-jeong followed them back to the factory.

"Have you been selling coffee in that way all along?"

다. 민영은 미정의 대답을 기다렸다. 노래가 그치고 정적이 흘렀다.

"무섭니?"

"응. 솔직히 그래."

민영의 대답에 미정은 고개를 끄떡거렸다.

"언닌 무섭지 않아? 감방 가는 거."

미정은 고개를 천천히 저었다.

"무서운 건 감옥 가는 게 아냐."

"그럼?"

"이 싸움에서 지는 거야."

미정은 눈을 감은 채 입술을 깨물었다.

"내가 감옥에 감으로써 우리가 이길 수만 있다면 난 평생이라도 가 있겠어. 아니 그 이상도 할 수 있어."

"어딜 쳐들어갈 거야? 사장집? 아니면 노동부장관실? 요즘 같으면 어딜 들어가든지 구속이겠지. 구속된다고 위장 폐업이 철회되는 것도 아니잖아."

미정이 자신의 머리칼을 움켜쥐었다. 그리고 미친 듯이 소리쳤다.

"억울해. 이대로 김세호한테 진다는 건 너무 억울해. 참을 수가 없어."

"It didn't start out that way. But then gradually we wanted to sell more so it developed into what you saw yesterday. But what's so wrong about doing it that way?"

Sun-ok stood up to Mi-jeong.

"What? You mean you still think it's ok? It didn't bother you one bit to see the girls acting like that? Are you street women? Were you trying to turn them into prostitutes?"

"Did it really hurt you so much to see us working? Or is it your injured pride talking?"

Mi-jeong gave Sun-ok a hard, penetrating stare.

As soon as it became known that the student workers' tuition had been paid for by the key money from the rooms rented by the president and secretary of the union, Sun-ok had taken the lead in insisting on earning money and paying them back. Mi-jeong wasn't against the idea. So far, they had passively accepted handouts from neighboring labor unions, students, and democratic organizations. But that kind of fundraising had only continued for a month or two. She felt quite proud of the union members who insisted they would earn the money themselves.

"What about the propaganda the company would

철순이 공장 지붕에서 떨어진 것은 노조를 결성하고 파업농성을 시작한 지 16일째 되던 날이었다.

꿈에 부푼 노조결성이었다. 다시는 동료를 선동하여 회사에 누를 끼치지 않겠다는 각서를 쓴 지 4개월 만이었다.

미정은 위원장에 뽑혔다. 철순과 민영은 사무장과 회계감사에 선출되었다. 요구사항은 간단명료했다. 어용노사협의회 폐지와 노조 인정, 일당 1,500원 인상, 강제 잔업 철폐, 이 세 가지였다.

세광 노동자들의 참여와 열기는 대단했다. 노동자들의 단결은 사장과 관리자들이 몇 년에 걸쳐 매일같이 다지며 억눌러온 질서를 단 하루아침에 뒤집어버렸다. 민주적으로 각성하고 노동자로서 단결한다는 것은 무서운 것이었다. 스스로 대표를 뽑고 스스로 규율을 만들고 스스로의 몫을 감당해나가는 새로운 질서를 만들어냈다.

노조결성 보고대회와 동시에 파업농성은 시작되었다.

그러나 공단에서 현금 재벌로 통하는 사장도 만만치 않았다. 구사대를 통한 폭력 탄압은 연대투쟁에 의해 실패했다. 사장은 장기전을 걸어왔다. 물량을 하청공장으로 빼돌리고 교섭에 응하지 않았다. 조합원들이 지쳐 떨어져 스스로 와해될 때까지 버티겠다는 의사를 노골화했다. 보

have made if they'd seen you last night?"

"Why is that so frightening? Does it matter?"

Mi-jeong stood up and walked over to the window. The union members on night-guard up on the roof of the canteen opposite had lit a bonfire and were singing. *Who made those people wield steel pipes, taller than themselves?* Mi-jeong quietly watched their images shimmering in the dancing flames. *Who made these kids cling on to the arms of total strangers trying to sell them a cup of coffee?*

The committee members sat slumped in their chairs, glancing up occasionally at Mi-jeong as she stood with her back to them staring out the window. Her raised collar made her look stubbornly determined.

"You think we *wanted* to act like that? We hate selling as though we're begging. We want to go back to work in the factory. We even miss the smell of paint thinner. Do you know how envious we feel when we see our classmates who are working in other factories arriving at school with their salary envelopes?" Sun-ok had a lot pent up inside.

Despite letters from Sun-ok and the labor union urging him not to, her father had turned up at the factory.

름이 지나도록 제대로 이루어진 교섭은 단 한 차례도 없었다.

조합원들은 초조하고 불안해하기 시작했다. 길어야 일주일이면 끝나겠지 했는데 타결될 전망이 조금도 보이지 않자 동요하기 시작했다. 변화 없는 상황에 지친 조합원들은 긴장이 풀렸다. 규율은 흐트러져 갔다. 낮에 몰래 빠져나가 돌아다니다 오는 조합원들도 한둘이 아니었다.

회사 측이 들여보낸 끄나풀은 집행부가 외부 세력과 연계되어 일부러 교섭을 않고 싸움을 길게 끌고 있다는 소문을 퍼뜨렸다. 그들은 지도부에서 밀려난 일부 남성 조합원들을 계속 들쑤셨다. 농성장 내에 술판을 벌였고 근거없는 시비를 걸었다.

한 번도 싸워본 경험이 없는 지도부로서는 어느 것 하나 쉬운 것이 없었다. 한결같이 며칠 사이에 얼굴이 몰라보게 여위었다. 특히 병약한 철순은 제대로 식사도 못 하여 보는 이들을 안타깝게 했다. 철순의 얼굴은 뼈가 앙상하게 드러났고 입술은 하얗게 갈라졌다. 눈은 퀭했으며 목소리는 잠겨 있었다.

언제까지 농성장에만 둥우리를 틀고 앉아 있을 순 없었다. 내부 분열과 와해를 노리는 사장의 교섭 지연 술책을

"What are you doing, demonstrating? What do you know about anything, when the blood on your forehead is still not dry? Demonstrating?"

Her white-haired father had slapped her hard across the cheek.

"But father, it's not like that..."

"Not like that? That writing scrawled in red on the wall over there—that's communist stuff! Go get your things packed!"

"We've done nothing wrong! I'd rather die than leave this place."

"How dare you?"

Sun-ok's father grabbed her by the hair. Mi-jeong tried to stop him, but it was no use. From the start the others had been watching the scene from the dorm's second floor. It was horrible.

"If that's the way you're going to go about it, we might as well just kneel before Kim Se-ho and surrender."

Mi-jeong raised her voice. Sun-ok leapt to her feet.

"That way, you keep saying, that way. What the hell's wrong with that way? Surely we need money to live on if we're to go on with this struggle! If you have a better idea, go ahead and tell us. Will you accept the 200 million *won* and put an end to it? I

분쇄하고 투쟁에 새로운 활력을 불어넣을 전기의 마련이 절실했다. 집행부에서는 '파업 기금 마련을 위한 연대집회'를 계획했다.

7월 16일로 예정된 집회가 하루 앞으로 다가왔고 조합원들은 준비에 박차를 가했다. 하루종일 현수막을 만들고 노래와 촌극을 연습했다. 나이 어린 조합원들이 풀통을 들고 공단을 돌며 안내문을 도배했다. 회사의 끄나풀들은 그 시간에도 수위실에서 술판을 벌였다.

"철순아, 너 하루종일 아무것도 안 먹고 그러다 쓰러진다."

미정이 현수막을 걸러 다니는 철순에게 기숙사 들어가서 쉬라고 말렸다.

"괜찮아. 이제 다했는데 뭐."

그 말이 미정이 들은 철순의 마지막 말이었다. 미정은 철순을 뒤로 하고 노래 준비를 둘러보러 갔다.

철순이 현수막을 걸기 위해 본관 옥상으로 올라간 것은 밤 9시가 넘어서였다. 이미 어둠이 내려앉은 뒤였다.

사장놈이 배짱이면 노동자님은 깡다구다, 현수막을 3층에서부터 바닥까지 늘어뜨렸다. 민영은 철순이 늘어뜨린 현수막의 끝에 돌을 매달아 고정시켰다.

won't betray Cheol-sun—even if it's for two billion, let alone 200 million."

"You listen to me! When did I ever say we were going to settle for money?"

The owner had proposed negotiations through the Labor Office. He had offered 200 million *won* in compensation to sixty-five of the union members. He also said he would publish letters of apology in two major newspapers for the union members' mental suffering. The Labor Office said it would take responsibility for getting all the union members re-employed elsewhere.

The union officers were unimpressed.

"Those bastards. They can reopen the factory with that kind of money."

The owner intimated that he might be prepared to increase the compensation figure. But he was adamant about never returning to normal operations.

"Apologies in newspapers? We've seen enough of those."

"Re-employed elsewhere? Any company owner who'd hire us, knowing we're from Segwang, would have to be out of his mind!"

But some of the union members were unsettled.

"마지막 하난데 어디가 멋질까?"

철순이 아래를 향해 물었다.

"그 옆에 그냥 걸고 내려와요. 날도 어두운데."

민영의 옆에서 도와주고 있던 조합원 하나가 소리쳤다.

"아냐. 마지막에 걸려고 남겨둔 건데, 멋진 곳에 달아야 지."

"뭔데?"

민영이 위를 보고 물었다.

"노동자의 서러움 투쟁으로 끝장내자!"

3층 옥상에서 외치는 철순의 잠긴 목소리를 민영은 알아들을 수 없었다.

"뭐라구?"

비상계단을 타고 내려온 철순에게 민영이 다시 물었다.

"노동자의 서러움 투쟁으로 끝장내자, 어디가 좋을까?"

"글쎄."

"저 굴뚝에 거는 게 제일 눈에 잘 띄지 않을까? 공단 어디서나 다 보일 걸. 어때?"

철순은 공장 지붕 위에 우뚝 솟은 굴뚝을 가리켰다.

"잘 띄기야 하겠지만 너무 높아서 어떻게 올라갈 수가 있어. 현장 지붕 위로 올라가는 계단도 없는데."

They did the math in their heads: 200 million *won* divided by sixty-five. That came to over three million per person. Sun-ok did the math, too. She knew that if her installment savings account, for which she had been putting aside fifty thousand *won* a month, was going to reach three million, it would take a full five years.

"What's so wrong with saying I'd rather earn and go on fighting, rather than accept dirty money?"

The sound of the door slamming behind her accompanied her last word.

In the end, it was Sun-ok's bank account that had prevented her from being dragged away by her father.

But father, we're not just doing nothing. Look. I've been saving fifty thousand a month for your sixtieth birthday celebration, but the owner has put an end to that. He's closed the factory doors in order to get rid of the union.

"Sun-ok's method of selling coffee went too far, I'll admit, but I reckon you were wrong to be so furious with her. What we must consider more significant is the unionists' determination to raise funds for the struggle by their own efforts."

It was the cultural affairs committee chair who had

"걱정 마, 내가 올라갈게. 이 날씬한 몸매가 있잖아. 저기 사다리나 좀 가져다줘."

조합원들이 본관 앞 바리케이드용으로 놓여 있던 사다리를 들고 왔다.

"내가 올라갈게."

민영이 나섰다.

"이 사다리나 잘 붙들어. 니들 같은 돼지가 올라가면 지붕 무너진다."

민영은 사실 굴뚝에 올라갈 자신이 없었다. 철순은 이미 사다리를 오르고 있었다.

"아이고, 그러다가 바람에 날려갈라."

사다리를 잡고 선 조합원들이 떠들었다. 사다리를 오르는 철순의 다리가 후들거리고 있다는 것은 그 자신밖에 몰랐다. 빈속이 울렁거렸다.

굴뚝은 공장 지붕 가운데 솟아 있었다. 철순이 슬레이트 지붕 아래로 추락한 것은 굴뚝을 향해 두어 발짝을 채 못 옮겨서였다. 슬레이트 지붕이 무너지면서 철순은 공장 속으로 떨어졌다. 낡아빠진 슬레이트 지붕은 철순의 야윈 몸뚱이 하나도 지탱할 수 없었던 것이다. 쿵, 소리를 듣고 민영이 현장 안으로 달려 들어갔을 때 철순은 이미 피를

spoken up.

"Let's drop the coffee-selling matter and focus on the company owner's proposal."

"Surely that's already been settled? We demand only one thing: re-start the factory. What else is there to say?"

The general affairs committee chair had interrupted the cultural affairs committee chair.

"It's not enough for us, the executive committee members, to say that we don't like the idea, that it won't do. That can't change what is into what isn't. The fact is that the union members are undecided. We have to understand what they're thinking first, it's not just what we think."

"So let's take the money, is that what you're saying? Speak clearly!"

"No, why do you keep repeating that? What I'm saying is that we have to find a way to unify the members since they are undecided."

Both voices were rising higher.

Min-yeong turned to Mi-jeong, who had come back to her seat and urged her to speak, "Why don't you say something?"

"It's true that there are some members who've been shaken by the owner's latest proposal. We're

훙건히 뿌린 채 증기가마 옆에 널브러져 있었다. 지원 나와 있던 선홍정밀의 대의원 하나가 민영과 조합원들이 울며 떠메고 나오는 철순을 받아 업었다. 선홍정밀의 대의원은 피가 뚝뚝 떨어지는 철순을 들쳐메고 큰길로 내달렸다.

달리는 택시 속에서 민영은 철순의 가슴에 귀를 대봤다. 심장은 희미하게 뛰고 있었다.

철순의 뇌수술은 시작한 지 1시간 10분만에 중단되었다. 집도를 맡았던 의사는 뇌의 파손이 워낙 심해 더 이상의 수술이 불가능하다고 밝혔다. 다시 봉합수술을 하고 자기 치유 능력에 따른 회생을 기대할 수밖에 없다는 것이 그의 설명이었다. 쓰러진 철순의 어머니도 중환자실로 옮겨졌다.

민영은 철순의 생명이 인공호흡기로 유지되는 이틀 동안 병실 문 앞에 쪼그리고 있었다. 이튿날 아침 한때 상태가 호전되어 인공호흡기를 떼어내기도 했다. 민영은 실낱같은 희망을 붙들었다. 그러나 철순은 끝내 회생하지 못했다.

소식을 듣고 달려온 지역의 노동자, 동료들의 눈물어린 간구도 소용없이 철순은 숨을 멈췄다.

1988년 7월 17일 밤 9시 45분, 마지막 말 한마디 남기

exhausted from the struggle, which has been going on for so long, and in fact there's no clear prospect that we can win."

As soon as the company heard that the union had rejected the 200 million *won* proposal, it turned to individual members.

If you leave now, we'll give you three million won. This is your last chance. After this, we won't give you a penny.

They visited the families and tempted them, too.

"If the company put forward a proposal that included such a considerable sum of money, it must be on account of the Labor Office's aim to keep the Segwang struggle from affecting wage-related strikes in the nearby area. From what I heard from a reporter, at a meeting where police, KCIA, and people from the Labor Office got together to discuss labor issues, they all saw Segwang's strike as a thorn in their side. Of course, their offer is itself a result of our fight. But if our ranks are dispersed at the sight of this small concession, then the last 150 days of struggle will have been for nothing."

"What about this idea?"

The publicity committee chair began, carefully weighing the effect of her words.

지 못하고 철순은 스물여섯의 나이로 한 많은 노동자의 삶을 마감하였다. 그녀가 떨어지는 순간까지 한끝을 놓지 않았던, 끝내 걸지 못한 현수막만이 뚫어진 지붕에 늘어 쳐진 채 유언을 대신했다.

'노동자의 서러움 투쟁으로 끝장내자!'

민영과 미정은 병실 문짝에 매달려 울었다.

철순의 시신은 영안실로 옮겨진 채 열흘을 보내야 했다.

넋을 잃은 어머님의 모습은 민영과 미정의 가슴을 무너지게 했다. 그러나 사흘 만에 겨우 기력을 차린 어머님의 태도는 철순의 어머니다웠다.

"우리 딸이 해달랬던 거 다 해놔. 우리 딸 남한테 손톱만치도 못 할 짓 한 적 없어. 내 보상금 한 푼 달라고 하지 않아. 우리 딸이 애지중지하던 저 애들 해달라는 거 다 들어줘. 안 그럴 양이면 우리 딸애 살려놓고 개한테 얘기해."

그러곤 다시 말을 잊었다. 빈소 앞에 넋을 잃고 앉아 있는 어머님을 보면 민영은 자신이 철순을 죽인 것 같아 견딜 수가 없었다.

경찰이 시신을 빼돌린다는 소문이 나돌았다. 민영은 매일 몇 구씩 들어오고 나가는 시신을 일일이 감시했다. 시

"Let's ask them for another 100 million to build a memorial for Cheol-sun. Because to be honest, I don't think it will be an easy task to reopen the factory, and wouldn't that be better than dragging this out, losing people one after another, and wasting it all."

"A memorial is not what Cheol-sun wanted," the general affairs committee chair commented.

A variety of opinions were expressed. It was difficult to reach any agreement. A few people said that victory was impossible, so it would be best to take the money and end it all. But everyone else wanted to go on fighting even if it meant they would all end up being arrested.

"This strikes me as a problem that can't be settled by a majority vote at an executive committee meeting. Let's take a week to review the outcome of today's discussion with the union members, and then decide. Each section should come up with a unanimous opinion by the evening of the last day of the Lunar New Year holiday."

The executive committee members left the meeting room without a word. Mi-jeong and Min-yeong were the only two left behind.

Mi-jeong collapsed into her chair. Min-yeong

신마저 저들의 손아귀에 빼앗기지는 말아야 했기에. 사장은 그 순간에도 조합원들을 동요시키기 위해 누가 밀지 않았느냐, 경찰에서 조합원들을 전원 잡아다 조사할 것이다, 위협을 했다.

철순의 어머님은 영안실을 지키고 있는 조합원들의 손을 말없이 잡아주곤 하였다. 사장은 철순의 죽음 앞에서도 의연했다. 대단한 사람이었다.

미정은 가슴이 죄어왔다. 멀쩡한 자식이 죽었고, 그 자식의 장례도 못 치른 채 영안실에 앉아 있는 어머님의 심정을 도대체 어떤 말로 표현할 수 있겠는가. 친척들은 보상비나 받고 장례를 치르라고 어머님에게 말을 건넸다. 회사와 경찰도 이웃을 통해 말을 넣었다.

미정은 아무 말도 할 수 없었다. 철순의 시신을 무더운 한여름에 영안실에 뉘어두고 싸웁시다. 그렇게 말할 수는 없었다. 죄인이 되어 어머님의 곁에 앉아 있을 수밖에 없었다.

영안실로 옮긴 지 7일째 되던 날 어머님은 열쇠를 꺼내 철순의 동생에게 건네주었다.

"집에 쌀 두 가마 있는 거 가져와라."

철순의 여동생은 무슨 말인지 알아듣지 못했다.

dragged the kerosene heater over to where Mi-jeong was sitting.

"Why don't you go and sleep?"

Mi-jeong lay back in the chair, her arms folded across her chest.

"You come with me."

Min-yeong crouched down by the stove, and stretched out her hands. The stove was barely warm enough to heat itself. The last seven months passed through Mi-jeong's mind like a movie. She hadn't known a day's peace since the organization of the labor union.

They now faced the final hurdle.

"You're having a hard time providing food for everyone, aren't you?"

"I feel bad for them. There's only kimchi and rice. Not even soup."

Union members no longer complained about the food. There was no more budget for side dishes. There was nothing but rice and kimchi. And if she did manage to get out to the market and produce an extra dish, that only made people angry. *We have so little money, why waste it like this?* And with the New Year, the members sensed that they were heading for a yet more intense battle.

"집에 쌀 두 가마 있는 거 가져오란 말이다. 한 가마는 공장에 애들 갖다주고 한 가마는 이리로 가져와. 애들도 먹어야 싸울 거 아냐."

한마디 한마디가 심장에서 나오는 신음이었다.

"나쁜 놈들."

미정은 죽는 순간까지 어머님의 이 저주를 잊지 못할 것이다.

장례식은 열흘 뒤에야 치러졌다.

송철순 민주노동자장, 태극기에 싸인 철순의 영구는 조합원들의 손에 의해 영안실을 출발하였다. 점심시간에 맞춰 장례행렬이 지난 공단가도는 7, 8공단의 노동자들로 메워졌다.

"여기 우리의 동지 송철순 민주노동열사가 떠나갑니다. 노동자의 서러움 투쟁으로 끝장내자, 외치며 떠나갑니다. 누구보다 이 7, 8공단을 사랑하였던, 노동자의 인간다운 삶을 갈망하며 싸우다 산화해간 송철순 동지가 여러분들에게 마지막 인사를 고하며 떠나갑니다."

검은 천으로 둘러싸인 선도방송차는 연도의 노동자들을 울렸다. 벗이여 고이 가소서, 삼기실업, 동일전자, 로얄공업, 청호산업 노동조합원들이 현수막을 앞세우고 공단

No one spoke openly, but they all felt they were facing a sacrifice, not only jail, but something beyond that as well.

"Mi-jeong, I want to ask you something personal. Promise you'll give me an honest answer?"

Mi-jeong nodded.

"You expect to go to jail, don't you?"

Mi-jeong remained silent, expressionless.

"Who else do you think will be going?"

The sound of distant singing reached them. The guard team on the rooftop of the building opposite was singing. The clock on the wall said it was past 2:20 a.m. Min-yeong waited for Mi-jeong to reply. The song ended, and all was silent.

"Are you scared?"

"To be honest, I am."

Mi-jeong nodded at Min-yeong's reply.

"Aren't you scared? Of going to prison?"

Mi-jeong slowly shook her head.

"Jail is not what scares me."

"What, then?"

"Losing this struggle."

Mi-jeong closed her eyes and bit her lower lip.

"If my going to jail meant that we would win this battle, then I wouldn't mind going in for the rest of

어귀어귀에서 철순의 운구를 맞이했다. 선홍정밀 노조원들도 전원이 작업복에 검은 완장을 하고 철순을 맞았다. 그들의 앞으로 펼쳐진 검은 현수막엔 이렇게 적혀 있었다. 해방의 불꽃으로 영원하라 동지여! 노동 해방의 그날에 부활하라 송철순 동지여, 선홍정밀 노동조합원 일동.

장례식은 그녀의 숨결이 구석구석 배인 세광물산 운동장에서 열렸다.

"철순아, 누구보다도 열심히 우리의 앞에서 싸웠던 철순아! 우리는 네가 무슨 말을 하고 싶어하는지 안다. 며칠을 견디지 못해 우리는 흔들리고 약해졌었다. 우리들은 너무 이기적이었고 나태했었다. 우리는 알게 되었다. 너의 죽음 앞에서조차 회개할 줄 모르는 가진 자들의 오만함과 어머님의 눈물 속에서 우리가 어떻게 해야 하는지 알게 되었다. 철순아, 이제 지켜보아다오. 세창의 깡순이들이 어떻게 싸우는지를. 넌 우리의 가슴속에 살아 우리가 내딛는 다리와 팔뚝 속에서 함께 할 것이다. 너는 노동자가 해방되기 위해 어떻게 싸워야 하는지 너의 죽음으로 가르쳐주었다. ……보아다오, 철순아. 우리의 전진을, 우리의 투쟁을, 우리의 승리를……"

미정은 추모사를 끝까지 읽어내려갈 수가 없었다.

my life. I would even do more than that."

"Are you planning to make a raid? The owner's house? The house of the Minister of Labor? The way things go these days, you'll go to prison whatever you do. And your going to prison won't stop them closing the factory."

Mi-jeong tugged at her hair. Then she cried out in anguish.

"It's so unfair! Kim Se-ho winning like this is so unfair. I can't stand it!"

Cheol-sun fell from the roof of the factory sixteen days after the labor union had been formed and the strike had begun.

Their union was founded with aspirations. It came four months after they had written pledges to the company that they would never again cause trouble to the company by stirring up their colleagues.

Mi-jeong was elected as the union president. Cheol-sun and Min-yeong were chosen as secretary and auditor. Their demands were clear and simple. They demanded three things: the abolition of the company-appointed labor council and recognition of their labor union; a daily raise of 1,500 *won*; and the abolition of obligatory overtime.

장례식을 마친 철순의 영구는 수출공단 본부 앞에서 노제를 지낸 뒤 장지인 경기도 마석의 모란공원으로 옮겨졌다. 전태일, 박영진, 성완희 열사가 잠든 묘역에 철순은 안장되었다.

공장엔 다시 기계 소리가 울렸다. 벽과 담벼락을 도배했던 구호와 요구사항들이 말끔히 지워지고 철순이 떨어졌던 현장 바닥의 핏자국도 씻겨졌다. 세광 조합원들의 가슴에 검은 리본이 달려 있는 것을 빼고는 예전과 다름없었다.

그러나 세광 깡순이들의 아픔은 이것으로 끝나지 않았다. 오히려 시련의 시작은 이때부터였다.

정상 조업의 재개와 동시에 폐업설이 현장에 떠돌았다.

28일간의 파업농성을 마친 조합원들은 평화로운 일터에서 동료를 잃어버린 상처를 아물리고 싶었다. 그러나 운명은 세광 깡순이들에게 가혹했다. 김세호 사장의 노조에 대한 적대 행위는 집요했다. 세광물산발전추진위원회란 반노조 조직을 만들고 그들로 하여금 탄압의 전면에 나서도록 하였다. 한편으로는 폐업설을 계속 흘려보냈다. 노조가 결성됐을 때 구사대로 나섰던 세광물산발전추진위원회의 구성원들은 술을 마시고 노조 사무실에 들어와

The participation and enthusiasm of Segwang employees were remarkable. Their solidarity was such that it took them only a single day to topple the oppressive system that the owner and the administrators had established and reinforced over several years. Their democratic awareness and their solidarity as laborers were a formidable combination. By choosing their own representatives and making their own rules, they created a new system in which they played their own part.

The strike started at the same time as the meeting announcing the establishment of a labor union.

However the owner, who was known as the "cash plutocrat" in the factories around, was no pushover. The attempt to break the strike by violence using the *kusadae* failed due to the support the workers received from the neighboring labor union. So the owner engaged in a long-term battle. He gave work to subcontracting factories, and refused to negotiate with the workers at his company. He made no secret of his intention to hang tight and wear out the unionists until they eventually collapsed. As a result, not a single attempt at real negotiations was made for fifteen days.

The strikers became increasingly impatient and

집기를 부수고 행패를 부렸다. 미정은 세발추(세광 깡순이들은 세광물산발전추진위원회를 이렇게 줄여서 불렀다)의 구성원들이 철순의 초상화가 놓인 조합 사무실에서 행패를 부리는 것에 대해 참을 수 없는 분노를 느꼈다. 그러나 인내했다. 노조는 최대한 인내를 결의했다. 회사의 사정을 공개하고 협조를 요청하면 생산량 증가에 노력할 의향이 있음도 분명히 했다.

세발추는 일당이 너무 많이 올라 회사가 망하게 생겼으니 임금을 도로 내리자는 것이었다. 어이가 없었다. 일단 3,720원에서 1,200원 올라 4,920원, 한 달 해봐야 147,600원이었다. 세광의 노동자들은 한 달 30일 일하고도 147,600원 받는 것마저 지나친 것이다.

김세호 사장이 바라는 것은 생산량의 증가도 임금의 인하도 아니었다. 그가 원하는 것은 노조의 해산과 조합원들의 퇴직뿐이었다.

그는 미정과의 단독 대담에서 자신의 의도를 숨김없이 드러냈다.

“회사 사정이 정말 어렵다면 그것을 공개하세요. 노조도 최대한 협조하겠습니다.”

“이것저것 떠나서 난 더 이상 장사하기가 싫어.”

nervous. They thought their strike wouldn't last longer than a week, but there was no end in sight, and they started to waver. With no change in the situation, the strikers started losing their tempers. Discipline broke down. More and more strikers secretly went out and roamed around during the day.

Company agents started to circulate a false rumor that the union representatives had joined up with outside forces and were deliberately not engaging in any kind of negotiations. They also stirred up discontent in some of the male workers who had been excluded from the executive committee. Drinking bouts occurred within the occupied factory and pointless quarrels broke out.

Nothing was easy for the executive committee members, who had no previous experience in this kind of struggle. Their faces grew gaunt in a matter of days. Cheol-sun, who had a weak constitution to begin with, was unable to eat properly and made her colleagues worry about her. Her facial bones began to stand out, and her lips were white and chapped. Her eyes became hollow and she lost her voice.

They couldn't stay cooped up in the occupied fac-

"사장님에겐 이 공장이 돈 버는 하나의 수단에 불과한지 모르지만 저희들에겐 생계가 걸린 일터입니다. 300명의 생계를 사장님 기분이 나쁘다고 짓밟을 수는 없잖아요."

"내 회사 내가 안 하겠다는데."

마침내 사장은 폐업을 선언했다. 합의서의 인주가 마르기도 전에 그는 합의 사항을 휴지 조각으로 만들었다.

김세호 사장은 노조의 요구사항에 대해 합의하고 정중한 사과문을 철순의 장례날인 7월 26일자 ㅎ신문에 게재까지 했었다.

근조, 송철순 민주노동열사. 지난 7월 15일, 파업농성 중 송철순 노동조합사무장이 지붕에서 추락하여 끝내 숨을 거둔 데 대하여 세광물산(인천 주안 7공단)의 사용주로서 고인의 영전에 깊이 사죄드리며 가족과 조합원들에게 사과를 표합니다. 기업을 운영하면서 노동자들의 절박한 요구를 절실하게 느끼지 못하고 소홀히 하여 파업이 장기화되고 급기야는 한 사람의 목숨까지 잃는 비극을 초래한 데 대하여 그 책임을 절감하며 앞으로 노동자들의 노동조건 향상에 최선의 노력을 다할 것이며 노동조합의 자유

tory forever. It was urgent to find a way to break through the owner's strategy of stirring division and disintegration by postponing negotiations, to find a way of giving their struggle a new burst of energy. The executive committee was planning a "Joint Fund-raising Rally."

The rally was planned for the 16th of July, and on the previous day the union members were busy with preparations. They spent the day preparing banners, rehearsing songs and skits. The younger members went round the complex with pots of glue, pasting up posters. At that moment, the company's agents were drinking in the guardhouse.

"Cheol-sun, you haven't eaten a thing all day, you'll collapse."

Cheol-sun was hanging up banners when Mi-jeong urged her to go back to the dormitory and rest.

"It's all right. I'm almost done."

Those were the last words that Mi-jeong heard from Cheol-sun. Mi-jeong turned around and went over to see how the songs were coming along.

It was past nine o'clock at night by the time Cheol-sun went up onto the rooftop of the main building to hang up banners. It was already dark.

If the goddam owner is audacious, the honorable

로운 활동을 전면 보장하겠습니다. 이제 우리 세광물산의 사용자는 노동조합의 요구사항에 대하여 전면 합의하고 고인의 장례를 치르게 되었습니다. 진심으로 고인의 명복을 기원하며 고인의 유지를 받들어 노조 활동에 성실히 협조할 것을 상심하고 계신 가족과 조합원들 그리고 고인의 운명을 가슴 아파하는 모든 분들께 엄숙히 약속 드립니다.

(주)세광물산 대표이사 김세호

그는 스스로 합의서의 조인식을 철순의 빈소 앞에서 갖자고 하여, 철순이 내려다보는 앞에서 제 손으로 서명까지 했었다.

조합원들이 분노한 것은 철순의 무덤에 흙도 마르기 전에 그의 시신 앞에서 한 약속을 짓밟은 김세호에 대한 배신감 때문이 아니었다. 폐업 선언을 한 그날이 바로 철순의 49재 날이어서도 아니었다. 조합원들의 가슴속에 쌓인 분노와 적개심을 폭발케 한 것은 철순의 찢긴 초상화였다.

사장의 폐업 선언에 따른 대책을 마련하기 위해서 전 조합원이 식당에 모여 있는 동안 회사는 조합 사무실에 비치된 철순의 초상화를 갈가리 찢어놓았다. 찢겨진 철순

workers are adamant. The banner scrolled down from the third floor to the ground. Min-yeong used stones to weigh down the bottom of the banner that Cheol-sun had let down.

"This is the last one—where should it go?"

Cheol-sun called down.

"Just hang it next to this one and come on down. It's already dark."

One of the strikers standing next to Min-yeong shouted up.

"No, I've been keeping this one for last—I have to find a good spot."

"What does it say?"

Min-yeong asked, looking up.

"End Workers' Grief with our Struggle!"

Cheol-sun shouted hoarsely from the third floor and Min-yeong could not understand her.

"What?"

Min-yeong asked Cheol-sun again as she was coming down the emergency stairs.

"End Workers' Grief with our Struggle! Where's a good place?"

"Hmm."

"I think it'll be most visible if it's hanging from the factory chimney, don't you? That way it'll be seen

의 대형 초상화를 부여안고 울부짖는 조합원들의 눈에선 불길이 타올랐다.

찢겨진 철순의 초상화를 앞에 놓고 49재를 지냈다. 철순의 어머니는 또 한 번 실신을 했다. 49재, 정상 조업에 들어간 지 꼭 1개월 만에 세광 깡순이들의 위장 폐업 분쇄 투쟁의 기나긴 막은 올랐다.

철순의 1주기 때 쓰려고 고이 접어두었던 피 묻은 현수막이 다시 내걸렸다.

미정이 올라갔다. 철순이 못다 오른 굴뚝 위로 올라가 현수막을 붙들어 맸다.

'노동자의 서러움 투쟁으로 끝장내자!'

세광 깡순이들은 다시 자신의 키보다 더 큰 쇠파이프를 들었다.

5

민영은 현장 문을 열고 들어갔다. 스위치를 올렸다. 천장 높이 매달린 수은등이 뿌옇게 불을 밝혔다. 성형실 복도에는 깨진 인형과 형틀이 널브러져 있었다.

민영은 작업대 한쪽을 짚고 인형 더미를 뛰어넘었다.

from every part of the complex."

Cheol-sun pointed at the chimney jutting high above the roof of the factory building.

"Sure, it'll be seen, but how are you going to get up that high? There aren't any stairs that go up there."

"Don't worry. I'll go up. I have a lovely slender body, don't I? Just bring that ladder over."

Several members carried over the ladder that was lying ready to be used as a barricade in front of the main building.

"Let me go up."

Min-yeong stepped forward.

"You just hold the ladder firm. The roof will collapse if you pigs go up."

The truth was that Min-yeong was scared to climb up. Cheol-sun was already on her way up ladder.

"Oh my, the wind will blow her off..."

The other unionists helping to hold the ladder were worried. Cheol-sun was the only one who knew how shaky her legs were as she climbed the ladder. Her empty stomach was heaving.

The chimney jutted out of the middle of the factory rooftop. Cheol-sun had barely advanced two steps toward it when she went through the roof. As

거쳐지나는 정형실도 마찬가지로 어지러웠다.

화공부 콘크리트 기둥에 붙은 스위치를 올렸다. 두 줄로 기다랗게 누운 작업대 위의 형광등들이 끔벅거리며 불을 밝혔다. 주임의 책상을 돌아 민영은 자신의 작업대로 갔다.

작업대에 손을 짚었다 떼자 손자국이 고스란히 찍혀났다. 의자에도 먼지가 두텁게 앉아 있었다. 손바닥으로 의자를 털고 앉았다. 도색을 기다리는 방망이곰들이 박스째 쌓여 있었다. 민영은 한 박스의 인형을 꺼내 작업대의 위에 가지런히 올려놓았다.

붓꽂이의 붓들이 뻣뻣하게 굳어 있었다. 민영은 신나통을 꺼내 용기에 부었다.

둥근붓과 5호붓을 신나에 빨았다. 말라붙은 팔레트도 씻었다. 다섯 달만에 맡는 신나 냄새가 짜릿했다.

다시 붓을 잡을 수 있는 날이 올까.

민영은 꼼꼼히 방망이곰의 몸체에 붓질을 해나갔다. 그리고 다리와 팔을 칠했다. 얼굴색을 올렸다. 곰인형의 표정이 살아났다. 눈을 그리고, 다음 인형으로 붓을 옮겨갔다.

민영의 손길이 점점 빨라져 갔다. 한 박스를 다 칠했을 때 민영의 코끝에는 땀이 송골송골 맺혀 있었다. 벽시계

the slates broke under her she fell straight into the factory. The old slate roof could not support so much as Cheol-sun's light weight. Min-yeong heard a heavy thud, and ran into the factory, where Cheol-sun was lying sprawled in a pool of blood next to the steam kiln. A volunteer from Seonheung who had been helping took Cheol-sun on his back, when Min-yeong and several other unionists emerged in tears, carrying Cheol-sun's body on their shoulders. Holding her firmly on his back, the volunteer from Seonheung went running out to the main road, her blood trickling to the ground.

Once in a speeding taxi, Min-yeong put her ear to Cheol-sun's chest. Her heart was beating faintly.

The operation on Cheol-sun's brain was stopped one hour and ten minutes after it began. The doctor explained that the damage to her brain was so severe that there was nothing further to do. He explained that all he could do was to stitch her up and trust to her own powers of recovery. Cheol-sun's mother collapsed and was hospitalized in the intensive care unit.

Min-yeong sat hunched in front of Cheol-sun's hospital room door for two straight days, as her friend was kept alive by an artificial respirator.

는 멈춰 있었다. 손목시계를 들여다보았다. 4시를 넘고 있었다.

결전의 날이 왔다.

철순이 맡았던 화공 2부의 작업대가 건너보였다.

출발 시간이 다가오고 있다.

오늘 낮엔 철순의 묘소에 다녀왔다. 철순에게 출정 인사를 했다.

가져간 사과와 배를 차려놓고 조합원들은 무덤 앞에 둘러섰다. 미정이 인사를 했다.

"철순아, 우리 왔어. 일어나봐. 자주 못 찾아와서 미안해. 아직도 싸움이 끝나지 않았어. 먹을 거 많이 못 사왔어. 돈이 별로 없어. 그래도 너 먹으라고 사온 거니까 많이 먹어."

조합원들의 눈언저리마다 물기가 배어났다.

민영은 철순에게 미안했다. 사과 3개, 배 2개, 북어 한 마리, 소주 한 병이 전부였다. 철순이 좋아하는 커피를 가져갔는데 버너가 고장나서 끓여주질 못했다. 하는 수 없이 찬물에 커피를 타서 주었다. 잔업을 하면 하루에도 대여섯 잔씩 커피를 마시던 철순이었다.

철없는 애들은 언제 울었나 싶게 사과와 배를 달라고

Cheol-sun's condition took a turn for the better the next day, and she was taken off the machine. Min-yeong clung to a faint thread of hope. But Cheol-sun failed to recover.

Despite the tearful prayers of her comrades and fellow workers, who all came rushing on hearing the news, Cheol-sun breathed her last.

On July 17, 1988, at 9:45 in the evening, Cheol-sun came to the end of her wretched worker's life, aged twenty-six, without speaking any last words. The banner that she had failed to hang up before she fell, dangling from the broken rooftop, stood in their stead.

End Workers' Grief with our Struggle!

Min-yeong and Mi-jeong clung to the door of her hospital room and wept.

Cheol-sun's body was taken to the mortuary, where it stayed for ten days.

The sight of Cheol-sun's mother so overwhelmed broke their hearts. But once she had recovered a little three days later, her mother exhibited a fervent ardor befitting her daughter.

"You do all that my daughter asked you to do! My daughter never hurt a soul. I'm not asking for a penny in compensation. Just you give these kids

미정을 졸랐다. 미정은 돌아가서 많이 사주겠다고 조합원들을 달랬다.

철순이 처음으로 조합원들에게 가르쳐주었던 노동해방가를 같이 불렀다. 그리고 조합원들은 새로 나온 노래를 철순에게 들려주었다. 동지여 내가 있다, 를 부르다 목이 메어서 민영은 마저 부를 수가 없었다.

"그날이 올 때까지/그날이 올 때까지/우리의 깃발을 내릴 수 없다/이름 없이 쓰러져간 동지들이여/외로워 마/서러워 마/우리가 있다/힘찬 깃발 휘날리며/나 여기 서 있다.

새날이 올 때까지/새날이 올 때까지/우리의 투쟁을 멈출 수 없다/싸우다가 쓰러져간 형제들이여/외로워 마/서러워 마/우리가 있다/찢긴 깃발 휘날리며/나 여기 서 있다."

성완희, 박영진, 전태일 열사와 문송면 군의 묘소에도 참배를 했다. 한 맺힌 죽음들은 철순만이 아니었다.

준비해간 빵을 나눠먹고 일기가 적힌 묘비 앞에서 기념사진을 찍었다.

'하루 평균 11시간의 노동, 거듭되는 피로에 쌓일 대로 쌓인 감정들과 지치고 야위어가는 몸. 신경은 점점 더 예민해져가 칼날처럼 날카로워지고 졸리고 피곤한 몸은 자

whom my daughter so cherished everything they're asking for. If you won't do it, bring my daughter back from the dead and talk to her!"

She said no more. Watching her friend's mother sitting in the mortuary reception room half-swooning, Min-yeong felt as if she had killed Cheol-sun herself. It was unbearable.

A rumor spread that the police were going to take away Cheol-sun's body. Min-yeong watched carefully as several corpses were carried into and out of the mortuary every day. She felt she had to prevent them taking away the body. Then the company owner tried to further unsettle the unionists by threatening them, suggesting that she had been pushed, that the whole group should be arrested and investigated.

Cheol-sun's mother kept going to every striker standing guard at the mortuary and squeezing their hands in silence. The owner himself showed no trace of emotion at Cheol-sun's death. He was quite somebody.

Mi-jeong's heart ached. She couldn't find words to express what Cheol-sun's mother must be feeling, sitting in the mortuary, her fine daughter dead, and unable to hold her funeral. Her relatives urged her

판기의 130원짜리 질 낮은 커피로 일으켜 세우고 거듭 쌓이는 노동의 피로로 몸은 썩어들어가는 듯하다. 이 자리에서 떨쳐버리고 일어설 용기가 없다면! 없다면, 하릴없이 노동만 하고 앉았는 노동자에 불과하다면, 착취의 선두주자인 자본가계급의 기름진 배를 더욱 기름지게 만들어주는 것 이상의 가치가 무어가 있는가!'

다시 방망이곰 한 박스의 칠을 끝냈을 때 시계는 5시 10분 전을 가리켰다.

민영은 붓과 팔레트를 깨끗이 씻어 가지런히 놓았다. 그리고 철순의 자리 앞으로 갔다. 철순의 작업대 위에도 뽀얗게 먼지가 쌓여 있었다.

'철순아, 이기고 돌아올게.'

민영은 손가락으로 먼지 쌓인 작업대 위에 썼다.

새벽 5시 정각, 조합원 전원이 식당에 모였다. 모두들 옷을 단단히 차려입었다. 식당 안은 팽팽한 긴장감이 감돌았다.

묵념. 정면에는 검은 액자에 담긴 철순의 영정이 놓여 있었다.

"조합원 동지들, 마침내 결단의 시간이 왔습니다. 150일 동안 싸워온 우리들의 투쟁은 승패의 갈림길에 섰습니

to take the compensation money and hold the funeral. The company and the police urged her to do the same, using her neighbors as their messengers.

Mi-jeong could find nothing to say. She couldn't urge everyone to fight on, leaving Cheol-sun's body lying in the mortuary at the height of the intense summer heat. She felt she was guilty, and could do nothing but sit by Cheol-sun's mother.

Cheol-sun's body had been in the mortuary for seven days when her mother took out a key and gave it to Cheol-sun's younger sister.

"Get the two sacks of rice we have at home."

Cheol-sun's sister failed to understand what she meant.

"I said: Get the two sacks of rice we have at home. Take one to the kids in the factory, and bring the other one here. These kids need food if they're to fight."

Every word came out like a groan straight from her heart.

"Wicked devils."

Mi-jeong felt she would never forget that curse as long as she lived.

The funeral finally took place after ten days had

다. 우리의 150일은 힘겹고 험난한 시간이었습니다. 그러나 그 150일 동안 흘린 땀과 눈물은 우리 모두를 위한, 우리 자신을 위한 것이었습니다. 우리 자신을 위한 땀흘림과 눈물을 아까워하지 맙시다. 우리가 아직 눈뜨지 않은 노동자였을 때 우리의 시간들은 오로지 사장을 위해 쓰여졌습니다. 그러나 우리가 인간으로 살기를 갈망하며 싸워온 지난날들은 비록 어렵고 고통스러웠지만 그동안 우리는 해방의 세상에 살았습니다. 사장은 우리를 돈으로 무릎 꿇게 만들려 하고 있습니다. 2억, 우리들에게는 상상도 할 수 없는 큰돈입니다. 우리의 영원한 동지 철순이는 단돈 1,500원을 더 받으려고 싸우다가 죽었습니다."

미정은 말을 끊고 천장을 쳐다봤다.

"2억, 너무나 큰돈입니다. 그러나 우리가 원했던 돈은 인간다운 삶을 이어나가기 위한 것이었을 뿐, 돈에 대한 탐욕이 아니었습니다. 우리는 부자가 되려고 했던 게 아닙니다. 인간답게 살고 싶었던 것뿐입니다. 김세호 사장이 내놓은 2억의 돈을 우리는 뿌리치기로 결의했습니다. 김세호 사장에게는 돈이 가장 소중한지 모르지만 우리에게는 돈보다 더욱 소중한 것이 있기 때문입니다. 동지에 대한 변할 수 없는 애정과 참 인간다운 삶이 중요하기 때

passed.

The casket of Song Cheol-sun, champion of the democratic workers' movement, wrapped in the national flag, left the mortuary carried by her co-workers. The funeral procession was timed to coincide with lunchtime, and many workers paid tribute as it passed down the road through sections seven and eight of the industrial complex.

"Song Cheol-sun, our comrade who gave her life for democracy is leaving us now! She is leaving us, crying out a message: End Workers' Grief with our Struggle! Our comrade Song Cheol-sun, who loved this seventh and eight complex more than anyone, and who died a heroic death so that laborers might live more human lives, is bidding you all a last farewell as she leaves."

A loudspeaker-car, wrapped in black crape, left all the zone's workers in tears. *Farewell, Friend*, preceded by banners, union members from Samgi Manufacturing Co., Dongil Electronics, Royal Industries, and Cheongho Co. greeted the hearse all the way through the industrial complex. All the workers from Seonheung Precision Mechanics, wearing black armbands over their working clothes, came out to hail Cheol-sun. The black banner flut-

문입니다. 우리는 이제 천만 노동자의 자존심을 보여주어야 합니다. 돈으로 되지 않는 게 있다는 것을 보여주어야 합니다. 우리의 가슴에 피눈물을 흐르게 하고 자신은 궁궐 같은 집에서 제 피붙이와 희희낙락 살게 내버려두지는 말기로 합시다. 이제 우리는 사랑을 말하지 않습니다. 이제 우리는 화해를 믿지 않습니다. 우리는 오직 불타는 적개심으로, 비타협적으로 싸울 뿐입니다."

미정은 조합원 하나하나를 둘러보았다.

"조합원 동지들, 우리는 승리해야만 이 자리에 다시 돌아올 수 있습니다. 김세호를 무릎 꿇려야만 현장에 들어가 다시 작업대에 앉을 수 있습니다. 이기고 돌아옵시다."

조합원 동지들, 사랑합니다, 며 미정이 말을 맺었다.

어두운 죽음의 시대 내 친구는 멀리 갔어도, 어깨를 걸고 나지막이 함께 노래를 불렀다. 토막초가 하나씩 나누어지고 불이 꺼졌다. 굵은 눈물 흘리며, 역사가 부른다.

미정부터 촛불과 함께 결단의 마음을 밝혔다.

"노동자의 눈물 없는 해방의 새날을 위해 온몸을 던져 싸우겠습니다."

민영이 촛불을 이어받았다.

"우리로부터 웃음을 빼앗아간 자들로부터 다시 웃음을

tering before them was inscribed: “Comrade, live forever as a flame of liberation! Comrade Song Cheol-sun, rise again on the day of workers' liberation!”

Cheol-sun's presence could be sensed in every corner of the Segwang sports-ground where the funeral ceremony was held.

“Cheol-sun! You led us in struggle more vigorously than anyone! Cheol-sun! We know what you wanted to say. Unable to endure for even a few days, we were faltering, growing weak. We were too selfish and lazy. But now, we know. We know what we have to do, because we've seen those arrogant people, incapable of repenting even in face of your death, and we've witnessed your mother's tears. Just you watch now. You'll see how the tough girls from Segwang can fight. You'll be alive in our hearts, you'll be with us in our arms and legs. By your death, you taught us how to fight for workers' liberation. Watch, Cheol-sun! Watch us move forward, watch us struggle, watch us win...”

Mi-jeong was unable to finish her eulogy.

When the funeral ceremony was over, Cheol-sun's hearse paused for a brief ceremony in front of the main office of the export division, and then drove

빼앗기 위해 싸웁니다."

"정상 가동이 되어 나도 친구들 앞에 월급봉투를 내밀고 싶다……"

"그동안 동료들을 사랑하지 못했습니다. 용서를 바랍니다."

65개의 촛불이 어둠 속에서 빛을 발했다.

순옥이 출정선언문을 읽어나갔다.

"김세호 사장, 또 다른 생명을 요구하는가! 더 많은 피를 요구하는가!

노동부, 당신들은 송철순 동지의 목숨 하나로는 아직 우리의 희생이 부족하다고 생각하는가! 더 큰 우리의 희생을 요구하는가!

당신들이 우리를 짓밟음으로써 열사의 뜻을 지워버릴 수 있다고 생각한다면, 2,500만 노동자의 자존심을 짓뭉개버릴 수 있다고 생각한다면, 그것이 얼마나 착각인가를 우리는 보여주겠다.

우리의 요구는 단 한 가지. 우리의 일터를 돌려달라!

이제 우리는 당신들을 2,500만 노동자의 이름으로 응징할 것이다!

우리는 선언한다. 죽을 수는 있어도 질 수는 없다!"

to the burial place, Peony Park in Maseok, Gyeong-gi Province. She was buried alongside other martyrs of the labor movement such as Jeon Tae-il, Bak Yeong-jin and Seong Wan-hui.

The factory once again echoed with the whirring of machines. Every signs of slogans and posters had been removed from the buildings and walls of the factory, and Cheol-sun's blood had been washed from the ground in the factory where she had fallen. Everything was as it had been before, except for the black ribbons that the Segwang union members wore on their chests.

That was not, however, the end of the suffering of the tough women of Segwang. Indeed, it was only the beginning of their ordeal.

At the very moment regular operation was resumed, word of a closedown began to spread through the factory.

The union members, who had finally reached the end of twenty-eight days of sit-in, longed for peaceful work place where they could tend the wounds caused by the loss of their colleague. But fate was cruel to the tough women of Segwang. The company's owner, Kim Se-ho, persisted in his hostile activities toward the union. He formed an anti-union

서로의 이름을 부르며 한 사람씩 돌아가며 악수를 했다.

모든 촛불을 껐다. 온통 어둠뿐이다.

낮은 노랫소리가 가슴에서 가슴으로 물결쳤다. 흩어지면 죽는다. 흔들려도 우린 죽는다. 하나되어 우리 나선다. 승리의 그날까지. 지키련다, 동지의 약속. 해골 두 쪽 나도 지킨다……

민영은 2조의 조장이 되어 정문을 빠져나갔다.

미정은 마지막 5조를 이끌고 세광을 나섰다.

캄캄한 새벽하늘에 펄럭이는 깃발들만 소리 없는 함성으로 이들의 출정을 배웅했다.

『내일을 여는 집』, 창비, 1991(1989)

organization called "The Segwang Development Committee," and then had them undertake an all-out campaign of intimidation. He also kept spreading rumors of a closedown. The members of the Segwang Development Committee, who had previously belonged to the *kusadae* when the union was first established, went on a drinking spree, invaded the union office, smashed the furniture, and generally misbehaved. The way the *sedeco* (that was the name the tough women gave those thugs, abbreviating the name of the organization) could have misbehaved in the office where Cheol-sun's portrait was hanging, filled Mi-jeong with uncontrollable rage. But she waited patiently. The union had decided to be extremely patient. They had made it plain that if the company made its state of affairs public and asked for the workers' cooperation, they would make every effort to increase production.

The *sedeco* claimed that wages had risen so much that the company was at risk, so they advocated lower wages. It was preposterous. Their daily rate had gone up by 1,200 *won* from 3,720 *won* a day to a total of 4,920 *won* per day, or 147,600 *won* a month. The way Segwang laborers were paid only 147,600 *won* for a full thirty days' work was excessive!

Kim Se-ho was not interested in increased production or lower wages. All he wanted was the abolition of the union and the exit of the union members from the factory.

He revealed his intentions to Mi-jeong plainly during a private meeting.

"If the company is really in a bad way, you should make it known publicly. The union will support you to the full."

"Never mind details. I just don't feel like doing business anymore."

"This factory may only be a means of making money for you, but for us it's the workplace on which our livelihood depends. Surely you can't trample on the livelihoods of three hundred people simply because you aren't in the mood?"

"I tell you it's my company, and I'll decide what to do with it."

He finally announced the closure of the factory. He had turned the agreement between the laborers and the company into a useless piece of paper before the ink was even dry.

Yet Kim Se-ho had agreed to the union demands, and had even published a respectful letter of apology in the H newspaper on the day of Cheol-sun's funeral, the 26th of July.

Sincere condolences. Song Cheol-sun, martyr for democratic workers' rights. On July 15th, in the course of a sit-in, Song Cheol-sun fell from the roof of the factory and met her death. As her employer at Segwang Manufacturing (Incheon Chuan Complex 7) I would like to extend my sincere apologies to the deceased, her family and colleagues. While directing my company I failed to recognize adequately the urgency of my employee's demands, and the strike went on until it resulted in the tragic loss of one person's life; I acknowledge my responsibility for this and undertake to make every effort to improve the conditions of the workers, guaranteeing the labor union freedom for its activities. Now all the union's demands have been accepted and the funeral of the deceased has been held. I wholeheartedly pray for the soul of the deceased, honor her last wishes, agree sincerely to allow union activities, and to her family members, unionists, and all those grieving over the fate of the deceased make this solemn promise.

Signed:

Kim Se-ho,

Chairman, Segwang Manufacturing

It was Kim Se-ho who suggested that the signing of the agreement take place in the mortuary before the funeral, and he signed the document with his own hand while Cheol-sun's portrait looked down at him.

The unionists' fury was not caused by Kim Se-ho's betrayal in breaking the promise he had made before Cheol-sun's dead body before the soil over her grave had even had time to dry. And it was also not even because the day the closedown was announced happened to be the 49th day after her death, a day of special ceremony. What caused the explosion of the fury and hostility accumulated in the unionists' breasts was the tearing up of her portrait.

While all the unionists were meeting in the canteen to discuss a counterplan after the announcement of the shutdown, people sent by the company tore up the portrait of Cheol-sun hanging in the union office. As the laborers hugged the shredded pieces of the large portrait, weeping bitterly, flames flared up fiercely in their eyes.

Placing the torn pieces of the portrait in front, they performed the ceremony for the 49th day. Cheol-sun's mother fainted again. On this 49th day, just barely one month after work had resumed, their long battle to return the factory to normal operations began.

They unrolled the bloodstained banner, which they had carefully folded up, planning to use it on the first anniversary of her death.

Mi-jeong climbed up. She climbed up the chimney that Cheol-sun had failed to reach and hung the banner.

"End Workers' Grief with our Struggle!"

Once again, the tough women of Segwang picked up steel pipes that were twice their height.

5

Min-yeong opened the factory door and went inside. She turned on the light. The mercury lamps dangling from the ceiling high above emitted a faint, milky light. The corridor in the molding section was littered with broken dolls and molds.

Min-yeong stepped to one side and jumped over a pile of dolls. The next room, the forms section, was in the same state of chaos.

She turned the light switch on the concrete pillar in the chemicals section. The neon tubes hanging by wires over the two long lines of worktables flickered as they came on. Min-yeong circled the desk of the manager, then made her way to her own workplace.

She placed one hand on the worktable and when she lifted it her hand had left a clear print. Dust was equally thick on the chair. She dusted the chair with a hand and sat down. Boxes of bears holding clubs stood in piles, waiting to be painted. Min-yeong took some out of a box and placed them carefully on the table.

The paintbrushes had hardened. Min-yeong took out the can of thinner and poured some into a pot.

She took a thick brush and brush number 5 and softened them in the thinner. She also cleaned off the crusted paint palette. It was five months since she had smelt the strong tang of thinner.

Will the day ever come when I'll be able to hold a brush again?

Min-yeong started to apply paint delicately to a club-holding bear's trunk with the brush. Next she painted its legs and arms. Then she colored its face.

The bear's expression came alive. She gave it eyes, and then she moved on to the next bear.

Min-yeong's hand started picking up speed. By the time she had painted an entire boxful, sweat was dripping down her nose. The wall clock wasn't working. She looked at her wristwatch. It was past 4 a.m.

The day of the decisive battle had come.

The worktable in division two that Cheol-sun had been assigned to was visible.

It would soon be time to set out.

The previous day they had visited Cheol-sun's grave to pay their respects before the battle.

"Cheol-sun! We've come! Wake up! We're sorry we couldn't come to see you more often. The battle isn't over yet! We couldn't buy much for you to eat. We don't have much money. But we've brought you something, so enjoy it!"

All the union members' eyes were streaming with tears.

Min-yeong felt apologetic toward Cheol-sun. All she had brought were three apples, two pears, one dried fish, and a bottle of *soju*. She had also brought instant coffee, that Cheol-sun used to like, but the portable burner was broken and she couldn't boil water. So she made coffee with cold water and offered it to her. Cheol-sun used to drink five or six cups of coffee a day when she worked overtime.

The others begged Min-yeong to give them the apples and pears, as if they'd forgotten all about their grief. Min-yeong comforted them by promising to buy a lot when they got back.

They sang in chorus the Worker's Liberation Song that Cheol-sun had first taught them. Then they sang their new song for her. Min-yeong managed "Comrade, I'm Here," but couldn't finish it because her throat was so dry.

Until that day comes,
Until that day comes,
We cannot lay down our banners.
Nameless, fallen comrades,
Don't feel lonely,
Don't feel bitter.
We are here.
I stand here,
Waving our powerful banner.

Until a new day dawns,

Until a new day dawns,
Our struggle can never cease.
Brothers and sisters, fallen in battle,
Don't feel lonely,
Don't feel bitter.
We are here.
I stand here,
Waving our tattered banner.

They also paid their respects in front of the graves of the heroic worker-martyrs Seong Wan-hui, Bak Yeong-jin, and Jeon Tae-il, as well as little Mun Song-myeon, the mercury poisoning victim. It was not only Cheol-sun who had died tragically.

They shared the bread they had brought with them, and took a photo of themselves in front of their comrade's tombstone, which was engraved with a page from Cheol-sun's diary.

Working an average of 11 hours a day, our bodies are consumed by accumulated exhaustion and emotion. We grow irritated and are easily upset as our bodies grow sleepy and weary; then a 130-won cup of bad coffee from a vending machine revives us, but the ever-accumulated fatigue from work seems grad-

ually to rot our bodies. If we don't have the courage to get out of here, to stand up for ourselves; if we just stay sitting helpless, doing our job, what are we doing but making ever fatter the fat bellies of the capitalists, great masters of exploitation?

By the time Min-yeong had finished painting the next box of bears, it was 4:50 a.m. by her watch.

She cleaned her paintbrushes and palate, and then put them back tidily in their place. Next she walked over to Cheol-sun's workplace. It too was covered with a layer of dust.

"Cheol-sun, I'll be back when we've won."

Min-yeong wrote with her finger in the dust on the table.

At precisely 5 a.m. all the strikers of the factory gathered in the canteen. They were all dressed in thick clothing. The air in the canteen was tense.

A moment of silence. A picture of Cheol-sun in a black frame was placed at the front.

"Union comrades! At last the decisive moment has come. Our 150 days of struggle has reached a cross-roads: victory or defeat. These past 150 days have been difficult and challenging. But the sweat and tears shed during those 150 days were shed for the sake of us all, for the sake of each and every one of us. Let us not regret a single drop of sweat nor a single tear! When we were still just workers with unopened eyes, our every hour was merely spent for the sake of our employer. But although the days spent fighting in the hope of living like human beings have been hard and painful, in those days, we have lived in a world of freedom. Our employer is trying to bring us to our knees with money. Two hundred million *won*! Big money that we can't even imagine! But our everlasting comrade Cheol-sun died fighting for just 1,500 *won* more!"

Mi-jeong stopped for a moment and looked up at the ceiling.

"Two hundred million *won* is big money. But what we wanted was just enough money for us to live as human beings, no more. We were never greedy for money. We never wanted to be rich. All we wanted was to lead human lives. We have decided to refuse the two hundred million that Kim Se-ho has offered. Money may be the most valuable thing for Kim Se-ho, but for us there are things that are more valuable. Unchanging affection for our comrades, and truly human lives are what really matter. Now we must show ten million workers' pride. We must show that there are things that money can't buy. Let us put an end to the way they force us to shed our blood and tears while they enjoy themselves with their families in palatial mansions. We will not talk about love any longer. We do not believe in reconciliation any longer. We will only fight, with blazing hostility, unyielding."

Mi-jeong looked at each and every union member.

"Union comrades! We can only come back here if we win this battle. We can only enter the factory and sit down at our work again if we bring Kim Se-ho to his knees. Let us win, and then return!"

She finished her speech with "My fellow co-workers, I love you all."

They locked arms and, in low voices, sang: "Even if my friend has gone far away in this dark age of death." They turned off the lights as small candles were passed around. "History calls us as we shed heavy tears."

Starting with Mi-jeong, as the candles glowed, resolute hearts came alive.

"I will fight with all my might for the new day of liberation when all workers will stop shedding tears!"

Min-yeong lit her candle from Mi-jeong's.

"Let us fight to retrieve our smiles from the hands of those who stole them!"

"I want to go back to work, then show off my wage envelope to my friends!"

"I've not shown true love all this time. I ask for forgiveness."

The light of sixty-five candles spread through the darkness.

Sun-ok read the "Declaration on Going into Battle."

Kim Se-ho! Are you demanding another life? Are you demanding yet more blood?

Ministry of Labor! Do you reckon that our sacrifice was not sufficient with comrade Cheol-sun's death? Are you demanding yet greater sacrifices?

You may think that you can crush our fervor by trampling us down, you may think you can crush the pride of 25 million workers, but we will show you how wrong you are.

We demand only one thing: Give us back our workplace!

We are going to chastise you now in the name of 25 million workers!

This we swear: though we may die, we can never

lose!

With that, they shook hands one by one, calling each by her name.

Then they blew out the candles. Darkness reigned.

A quiet song passed from heart to heart: "If we scatter, we die. If we waver, we die. We advance as one. Until the day of victory. We will be faithful to our comrade's oath. Faithful even if our skulls are split in half..."

Min-yeong stepped out of the front gate, leading the second division.

Mi-jeong headed the fifth division, the last, and walked out of Segwang.

The banners flapping in the dark dawn sky sent them off to battle with a voiceless war cry.

1) "Eonni" means older sister. In Korean, women often call an older female friend "Eonni."

Translated by Dafna Zur and An Son-jae

해설

Afterword

사랑, 불가능한 꿈을 좇는 모험

홍기돈(문학평론가)

근대 체제가 작동하기 위해서는 하나의 전제가 필요하다. 생산물은, 생산자의 소비가 아닌, 판매를 위하여 생산되어야 한다는 것. 따라서 아무런 생산 수단을 가지지 못한 근대인이라면 제 자신의 육체라도 노동력의 형태로 판매해야 한다. 이마저 거부당한다면 먹고살 가능성은 여지없이 박탈당하고 만다. 반면 노동력을 사들인 자본가는 노동력과 생산 수단의 결합으로써 더 많은 이윤을 기대할 수 있게 된다. 그러니까 노동자는 자본가에게 이윤을 창출하는 수단으로 존재한다는 것이다. 노동자와 자본가는 그런 방식으로 관계하고 있다. 「새벽 출정」은 이러한 사실 위에서 펼쳐지기 시작한다.

Love, the Risk of Pursuing Impossible Dreams

Hong Gi-Don (literary critic)

For modern systems to function, one prerequisite is required: products have to be produced for sale, not for consumption by those producing them. Thus modern people, having no means of production of their own, are obliged to sell their own bodies in the form of labor. If people are denied this, they are deprived of the very possibility of survival. On the other hand, the capitalists who purchase people's labor can expect higher profits by combining labor with the means of production. In that way, laborers exist as a means by which to generate profits for the capitalists. That's how laborers and capitalists are related. "Off to Battle at Dawn" begins with that

먼저 노동자의 입장에서 살펴보자. 7년 동안 세광물산에 출근하였던 '민영'은 잔업 특근을 거부했다가 사직서를 받아들게 된다. 이 순간 그녀의 존재 방식은 선명해진다. "너는 일당 4,080원짜리 고용인 이상의 그 무엇도 아니야. 그리고 이제 사장은 네가 필요 없어졌어. 매일 구매하던 4,080원짜리 물건을 이제는 다른 곳에서 구입하겠다는 거야." 반면 자본가가 회사를 운영하는 목적은 애초부터 이윤 추구였다. 그러니 사장 '김세호'가 이제껏 그러한 길을 따라온 것은 당연하다. "처음 시작할 땐 하나뿐이던 건물은 다섯 동으로 늘었고 6기뿐이던 가마도 20기로 늘었다. 생산직 사원도 70명에서 300명을 넘어섰다. 해가 가도 불지 않는 것은 얇은 월급봉투뿐이었다."

자, 이제 두 개의 세계가 충돌한다. 「새벽 출정」의 미덕은, 이는 방현석 소설 전반에 나타나는 특징이기도 한데, 계급투쟁이 구체적인 사건들을 통해 재현됨으로써 생동감 획득에 성공한다는 점이다. 농성장을 떠나는 동료들, 농성장 내부의 갈등과 긴장, 생산량 증가를 유도하는 사용자 측의 전략, 농성하는 이들에게 가해지는 학교와 집 등에서의 압박, 위장 폐업으로 갈등을 회피하고 정리하려는 사장의 선택 등. 노동 현장을 다루는 소설이 방현석 출

fact.

First, let us see things from the laborers' viewpoint. Min-yeong, who has been working at Segwang Manufacturing Inc. for seven years, refuses to do overtime and is given a resignation letter to sign. At that, her form of being becomes clear to her: "You're nothing more than a position worth 4,080 *won* per day. The owner doesn't need you any longer. Now he's going to go somewhere else to buy the object he paid 4,080 *won* for each day." By contrast, the capitalist's purpose in running the company was from the start to make a profit. The path taken by the owner Kim Se-ho is only natural: "When they started working there, the factory consisted of one building only; now there were five, and the number of kilns also grew from six to twenty. The number of productive workers also increased from seventy to over three hundred. The only thing that never seemed to expand from year to year was the thin envelope that contained the wages."

In this way two worlds collide. The virtue of this story is a characteristic feature of Bang Hyeon-seok's entire oeuvre: class warfare, by being depicted through concrete incidents, is successfully brought to life. Comrades who leave the occupied

현 이전과 이후로 나뉘는 이유가 여기에 있다. 그는 자신의 현장 체험을 바탕으로 하여 이전의 생경한 관념성을 뛰어넘어 계급의식이 분출하는 구체적인 상을 제시해 내었다. 「새벽 출정」은 이러한 사실을 확인시켜주는 대목에서 빛을 발한다.

위의 사실이 방현석 소설 전반에 걸쳐 있는 특징이자 장점이라면, 「새벽 출정」은 여러 노조들이 지역 단위로 굳건하게 연대하여 투쟁에 나서는 면모를 부각시키고 있다는 점에서 다시 변별된다. 이를 이해하기 위해서는 작품이 발표되었던 1989년 봄 즈음의 상황을 뒤돌아볼 필요가 있겠다.

'한강의 기적'으로 표현되는 남한의 놀라운 경제 성장의 뒷면에는 노동자들의 막대한 희생이 있었다. 세계 최장 시간 노동은 물론 그 위에 잔업, 특근까지 얹혔으며, 그에 따른 정당한 대가의 요구는 좌익 세력의 준동으로 몰아세워졌다. 언론, 종교단체, 학교기관 등이 이러한 흐름에 동조하였다. 여기에 변화가 일기 시작한 시점이 '1987년 6·7·8 노동자 대투쟁'이었다. 이때부터 노조가 설립되기 시작했으며, 노동 시간 단축이라든가 임금 인상도 자본가와 비로소 논의가 가능해졌다. 그러니까 1989년 봄이

factory, stresses and conflicts inside the factory, the strategies used by employers demanding increased productivity, the pressure brought to bear on the strikers by schools and families, a disguised shutdown, the choice made by the owner to avoid conflict and settle matters, etc. Herein lies the reason why we divide novels that focus on the workplace into those that were published before and after Bang Hyeon-seok began writing. Taking his own working experience as a starting point, and going beyond immaterial abstractions, he depicts concrete images issuing directly from class-consciousness. "Off to Battle at Dawn" shines because of this achievement.

This feature is a distinguishing characteristic and strength of all Bang Hyeon-seok's fiction. "Off to Battle at Dawn" is also distinguished by the way it depicts members of various local unions uniting in a common struggle. In order to understand this, it is necessary to recall the situation in the spring of 1989, when the work appeared.

Underlying the amazing economic growth known as the "Miracle of the Han River" were the enormous sacrifices endured by the laborers. Laborers actively advanced demands for a reasonable wage

라면 사회적으로 고립되었던 노동자들이 서서히 결집하면서 연대투쟁을 통해 위상을 높여나가던 시절이 된다. 「새벽 출정」은 그러한 현실을 오롯이 담아내고 있는 셈이다.

발표된 지 20년 이상이 지났지만 「새벽 출정」의 세계는 여전히 낡지 않은 모습으로 생생하게 다가온다. 노동자와 자본가의 관계는 어떠한 수정도 없이 요지부동 작동하고 있으며, 신자유주의의 공세가 날로 거세지는 데 따라 「새벽 출정」의 세계가 반복되는 양상으로 현실이 펼쳐지고 있기 때문이다. 그렇다면 탈출구는 어떻게 마련해가야 하는 걸까. 작품의 마지막 부분에서 노조위원장 '미정'이 동지들을 선동하는 가운데 "돈으로 되지 않는 게 있다는 것을 보여주어야 합니다."라는 문장이 나타난다. 이게 과연 가능한지 답변은 저마다 다르겠으나, 분명한 사실은 하나 있다. '돈으로 되지 않는 것'의 가치와 존재를 보여주지 못한다면 「새벽 출정」의 세계는 마치 '햄릿의 유령'처럼 언제고 우리 앞에 귀환할 것이라는 점.

체 게바라가 제안했다. "우리 모두 리얼리스트가 되자. 그러나 가슴속에는 불가능한 꿈을 가지자." 「새벽 출정」의 노동자들은 불가능한 꿈을 가슴에 품은 리얼리스트들이다. 그들 역시 체 게바라와 똑같은 자리에 서서 말을 걸

corresponding to the longest working hours in the world that became even longer because of extra hours and overtime, but these demands were blamed on agitation by leftist forces. The media, religious groups, and educational institutions aligned themselves with labor movement. What marked the start of a change was the "Great Workers' Struggle" of June-August 1987. From that point on, labor unions were formed and it became possible to negotiate with the capitalists about reducing working hours and raising wages. The spring of 1989 was the moment when the laborers, who had previously been socially isolated, began to unite and raise the stature of their struggle. "Off to Battle at Dawn" fully reflects this new reality.

It has already been more than twenty years since "Off to Battle at Dawn" was first published, but the world depicted in this story has not aged and remains vivid. That is because relations between laborers and capitalists remain unchanged, while the thrust of neoliberalism grows fiercer daily. The world depicted in "Off to Battle at Dawn" remains today's reality. So what escape can there be? In the last section of the story, we find the labor leader Mi-jeong encouraging her comrades and saying, "We

어오고 있다.

must show that there are things that cannot be turned into money." Everyone will have a different idea as to whether this is possible or not, but one thing is clear: if we cannot show the value and reality of "things that cannot be turned into money," the world of "Off to Battle at Dawn" will keep coming back to haunt us like Hamlet's ghost.

Che Guevara suggested, "Let's all become realists, but with impossible dreams in our hearts." The laborers of this story are realists with impossible dreams in their hearts. They stand side-by-side with Che Guevara and transmit the same message.

비평의 목소리

Critical Acclaim

「새벽 출정」을 다시 읽었다. 지금보다는 순수했을 때, 그때 이미 시대는 '혼돈' 속으로 빠져들고 있었지만, 그래도 버텨야 한다고 생각했을 때, 그때 「새벽 출정」은 얼마나 커다란 위안이 되었던가. 어제로부터 오늘을 지나, 내일까지도 끝없이 펼쳐진 것만 같은 고통을 느끼면서도 민영이는, 미정이는 캄캄한 새벽 출정을 나섰다. 그랬다. 방현석이, 그가 그녀들로 하여금 패배하지 않으리라는 어떤 보장도 없이 쓰고 있었을 때, 그녀의 운명은 마치 '우리'의 운명과 같았다. '우리'가 얻고자 하는 것은 야만의 법칙이 지배하는 세계 속에서의 한 단계 상승이 아니라, "동지에 대한 변할 수 없는 애정과 참 인간다운 삶"임을 확신했던

Recently I reread "Off to Battle at Dawn." How comforting it was to read back in a time when we were purer than we are now, when we wanted to withstand an era that was plunging into total "chaos"! Min-yeong and Mi-jeong went off to battle at dawn in the midst of darkness and pain that seemed destined to continue for numerous tomorrows. That's right. When Bang Hyeon-seok was writing about his characters without guaranteeing their success, their fate felt like "our" fate. To firmly believe that we wanted not a step up in a world governed by barbaric rules but "an unchangeable love toward our comrades and a truly human life,"

것, 그랬기에 숨을 막아드는 불안에 시달리면서도 떠나지 않으면 안 된다는 결단에 몸을 맡겼던 것, 그것이 '우리'의 '어제' 아니었던가. 그리하여 「새벽 출정」의 마지막 쪽을 넘겼을 때, 다가오던 서늘한 감동은 슬픔이 무엇인지 아는 자, 공포가 무엇인지 아는 자의 그것이었다.

방민호

방현석의 작품이 지닌 가장 두드러진 특징 중의 하나인 비장함은 그가 가지고 있는 튼튼한 현실 인식에 그 뿌리를 두고 있다. 궁극적인 승리와 가능한 현실적 실패 사이에서 균형 감각을 가지고 현실을 그려낼 수 있기 때문에 그는 안일한 현실 인식에 입각한 행복한 결말을 피할 수 있는 것이다. 이러한 현실 인식은 또한 그의 작품을 단순한 혁명적 낭만주의가 아니라 과학적 세계 인식에 기초한 혁명적 낙관주의의 가능성을 품은 작품으로 돋보이게 하는 것이다.

김재용

방현석의 첫 작품 「내딛는 첫발은」이 발표되었을 때, 당연히도 우리는 멀리는 전태일의 죽음으로부터 1980년 5

and therefore to entrust ourselves to our resolution to go off to battle even in the midst of sickening anxieties—wasn't that our yesterday? Thus those of us who knew what sadness was and what fear was felt simultaneously chilled and moved when we turned the last page of "Off to Battle at Dawn."

Bang Min-ho

Tragic heroism, one of the most prominent characteristics of Bang Hyeon-seok's works, is based on his solid grasp of reality. He avoids a happy ending based on easy optimism, since he has a sense of balance between ultimate victory and actual defeat in the present. Thanks to this solid grasp of reality, Bang's works stand out as bearing revolutionary optimism based on a scientific worldview rather than an easy and groundless confidence.

Kim Jae-yong

Bang Hyeon-seok's first work, "The First Step," naturally reminded us of the history of "labor literature" from the time of Jeon Tae-il's death through the May Uprising in 1980 to the publication of *Dawn of Labor.* Bearing the burden of this progressive history, Bang's literature depicts the everyday

월 광주항쟁과 『노동의 새벽』을 생생한 이념으로 하고 있는 '노동문학'의 역사성을 떠올리지 않을 수 없었다. 이 진행하는 역사성을 감당하면서 노동 현장의 투쟁하는 일상을 그려낸 것이 방현석의 문학이었다. 방현석은 그의 작품들에서 그 투쟁이 좁게는 작업장 단위의 패배로 귀결될 수밖에 없는 경우에도 연대의 힘을 확인하고 쌓아가는 긴 희망에 오늘의 패배를 넘겨주는 의연한 낙관을 전해주었다. 그런데 이런 전언들을 누구나 고개를 끄덕일 수 있는 사람들의 이야기로 형상화해낸 데 방현석의 작가적 역량이 있었다. 가령 한 해고 노동자의 복직 투쟁을 다룬 중편 「내일을 여는 집」에서, 다시 봉제 공장에 나가게 된 아내를 대신하여 젖먹이 딸을 어린이집에서 데려오는 해고 노동자 성만의 긴 귀갓길 발걸음을 복직 투쟁의 지친 내면에 한발 한발 겹쳐놓은 대목의 섬세함은, 노동 문학이 어떤 이념의 선취에 의해서가 아니라, 사람살이의 소외와 연대를 생활 세계와의 연관 속에서 붙잡아 드러내는 깊고 따뜻한 시선에 의해 쓰여지는 것임을 확인시켜주었다.

정홍수

자본의 내부에서 그 외부를 엿보기는 논리적으로 불가

struggles confronting workers in their workplaces. Even when these struggles are defeated in individual workplaces, Bang is the messenger of steadfast optimism who transforms today's defeat into the far-reaching hope that comes from confirming and gathering the power of solidarity. Bang's talent as a writer shines in his ability to embody his messages in stories to which everybody can relate. In Bang's novella "House Opening Future," a story that deals with a fired worker's struggle for reinstatement, take a look, for example, at the description of Seong-man's footsteps on the way back from the childcare center where he picked up his baby daughter because his wife had begun working at a sewing company. We see in this exquisite description of Seong-man's footsteps, which reflect his mood, exhausted from the lengthy struggle for reinstatement, that the author did not write his stories based on some ideology but from the perspective of a profound and warm understanding of and concern for the lives of the marginalized and their solidarity.

Jeong Hong-su

It is logically impossible to have a glimpse of what lies outside the capital from within the capital. It is

능하다. 더구나 자본의 내부에서 그 외부를 살아간다는 것은 더더욱 불가능하다. 이 불가능한 길, 없는 길을 걸어가는 것이 방현석의 문학적 역설이다. 그러나 해답이 없지는 않다. '세계=나'가 되기를 꿈꾸는 자에게 중요한 것은 어떤 '흐름'이 되는 것이며, '주체(이끄는 자 혹은 가르치는 자)'가 되는 것이 아니기 때문이다. 그가 가는 곳이 길이 되는 것이 아니라, 그는 스스로 길이 되려 한다. 미래를 소유할 수 있는 사람은 없다. 소유나 통제 자체가 원천적으로 불가능한 미래로부터 우리는 희망을 빌려온다. 또 다른 다큐멘터리언이 되고 또 다른 여행가가 됨으로써, 즉 비(非)작가가 됨으로써, 방현석은 다시 작가의 길로 돌아올 것이다. 그는 문학의 영토를 강력하게 이탈하고 나서야 비로소 그 어느 때보다도 문학에 가까워졌다. 그가 귀환한 문학의 영토가 응고되지 않는 길은 그가 무한히 떠나는 길밖에 없다.

정여울

even more impossible for someone to live outside of the capital within the capital. To walk on this impossible, non-extant road is the paradox of Bang Hyeon-seok's literature. But it is not entirely impossible for us to explain this. What's important to the person who dreams of achieving "World=I" is to become part of a certain "current," not its "subject (a leader or a teacher)." Bang Hyeon-seok wants to become a road rather than walk on the road. Nobody can own the future. We borrow hope from a future that nobody can own or control. By becoming another documentarian and traveler, Bang Hyeon-seok will come back to the road of a writer. He became closer to literature by intentionally and forcefully deviating from its territory. In order not to calcify the territory of literature wherever he returns, he has to forever leave.

Jeong Yeo-ul

방현석

작가 방현석은 1961년 경남 울산에서 출생하였다. 1980년 중앙대학교 문예창작학과에 입학하였으며, 아직 졸업하기 전인 1985년 신분을 숨기고 인천의 한 공장에 노동자로 취업하였다. 1980년대는 흔히 '불의 시대'라 일러지는데, 이는 정치 민주화·경제 민주화 투쟁이 그 시기에 폭발적으로 일어났음을 상징적으로 나타내는 표현이다. 이러한 시대 분위기 속에서 소설 분야에서도 노동자의 당파성에 입각한 작품들이 발표되기 시작하였으나, 구체적인 형상화에 도달하지 못한 채 이념만을 거칠게 강조하는 수준을 넘어서지 못하는 한계가 두드러졌다. 1988년 《실천문학》 봄호에 발표된 방현석의 등단작 「내딛는 첫발은」이 단번에 주목을 받았던 까닭은 바로 그 한계를 뛰어넘었기 때문이었다. 노동자의 당파성을 견지하되, 생동감 넘치는 인물들을 창조해내는 한편 숨 막히는 대결의 순간을 긴장감 있게 조성해내는 능력은 그의 현장 경험에서 길러졌다고 볼 수 있다. 이러한 장점은 첫 번째 소설집 『내일을 여는 집』 전체를 관통하고 있으며, 방현석은 이로써 1980년

Bang Hyeon-seok

Bang Hyeon-seok was born in Ulsan, Gyeongsang-nam-do in 1961. He entered the Department of Creative Writing at Chung-Ang University in 1980, and got a job as a laborer with an assumed identity at a factory in Incheon in 1985 before he graduated from college. The 1980s is often called the "time of fire," symbolizing the fiery political and economic democratization movement during that era. Poems and stories written from the perspective of laborers were published, but most failed in concretely embodying the partisan ideology they tried to represent. "The First Step," Bang Hyeon-seok's debut story published in the spring 1988 issue of *Silcheonmunhak*, immediately attracted critical attention by succeeding in this task of concrete embodiment. It seems that he honed his skill to create lively characters and portray breathtaking moments of conflict without falling into the pitfalls of the abstract presentation of ideological schemata during his time at factories. *House Opening Tomorrow*, his first collection of short stories, is con-

대를 대표하는 소설가로 자리매김하였고, 제9회 신동엽창작기금을 받기도 하였다.

하지만 1990년대에 접어들면서 국내외의 정세는 급박하게 변모해 나갔다. 세계사적인 차원에서 보자면 1991년 말 벌어진 소비에트 연방의 해체가 심리적 동요를 일으키는 원인으로 작용했으며, 국내적으로는 군벌정치의 종식에 따른 절차적인 민주주의의 도입이 투쟁의 동력을 상실케 하는 근거가 되었다. 이후 밀어닥친 신자유주의의 영향 속에서 민주 노조 역시 점차 균열을 드러내기 시작하였다. 1994년 공장을 떠난 방현석은 전국의 노동운동 현장을 찾아다니며 민주 노조의 역사와 현실 기록에 나섰는데, 1999년 펴낸 산문집 『아름다운 저항』이 그 결과이다. 이 시기에 내놓은 대표적인 작품으로는 장편소설 『십년간』 『당신의 왼편』을 꼽을 수 있다. 두 작품은 모두 현재 상황의 모태가 되는 전사(前史) 탐구의 성격이 짙으며, 『십년간』은 1970년대의 한국 사회를 대상으로 삼고 있고 『당신의 왼편』이 1980년대의 양상을 다루고 있다.

시대의 조류로부터 거리를 두고 있던 방현석이 다시 문단의 중심에 우뚝 선 것은 「존재의 형식」을 통해서이다. 2002년 겨울 발표된 이 작품은 「겨울 미포만」 이후, 중단

sistent with his achievement in "The First Step," and catapulted Bang to the status of one of the most representative fiction writers of the 1980s. He was awarded the ninth Shin Dong-yeop Creative Writing Fund for this book.

The 1990s were different times, though. Internationally, the dissolution of the Soviet Block brought psychological turmoil to activists, and internally, they lost momentum for a continued fight after the establishment of procedural democracy at the end of the military regime. Democratic labor unions were also fractured by the violent wave of neo-liberal capitalism. After leaving a factory in 1994, Bang Hyeon-seok collected history and the current state of democratic labor unions by visiting labor movement scenes all over the country and published *Beautiful Resistance*, a prose collection, in 1999. During the same period, he published two novels, *A Decade* and *Your Left Side*. Both novels reflect on the history behind the 1990s, *A Decade* being the history of the 1970s and *Your Left Side*, the history of the 1980s.

Bang Hyeon-seok occupied the center stage of the literary scene by publishing "Forms of Being" in the winter of 2002. This novella broke Bang's more than

편소설로만 치자면, 5년 이상의 침묵을 깨고 선보인 중편이다. 사업장 안에서 벌어졌던 노사 갈등은 이제 국경을 넘어 국가 단위로 펼쳐지고 있고, 지난날 한국에서 학생운동을 했던 인물들은 졸업 이후 각각의 길을 걷고 있으며, 세상의 혼란한 변화 속에서도 과거에 품었던 이상을 여전히 간직하고 있는 베트남인 '레지투이'가 등장한다. 비루한 현실 속에서도 꼿꼿하게 빛나는 영혼의 존재 방식을 제시한 이 작품으로 작가는 2003년 오영수문학상, 제3회 황순원문학상을 수상하였다. 「존재의 형식」뿐만이 아니라 이어서 발표한 중편소설 「랍스터를 먹는 시간」 그리고 산문집 『하노이에 별이 뜨다』 등으로 판단한다면, 이 시기 그의 세계에서 '베트남'이 성찰의 계기로 얼마나 중요하게 작용하는지 확인할 수 있다.

방현석의 문단 활동으로는 《실천문학》 편집위원을 역임한 바 있으며, 현재 《아시아》 편집 주간을 맡고 있다는 사실이 정리될 만하고, 현재 중앙대학교 문예창작학과 교수로 재직 중이라는 점도 부기할 필요가 있겠다.

five-year silence after his publication of "Mipo Bay in Winter," if we count only his short stories and novellas. The conflict between capital and labor now changes its scene from within a company to between countries. Previous student activists have been going their separate ways since graduation, and there is Le Chi Thui, a Vietnamese who continues to pursue his ideal in a changed and confusing world. Bang received the 2003 Oh Yeong-su Literary Award and the third Hwang Sun-won Literary Award for this novella. He then went on to publish "Time to Eat Lobster," another novella set in Vietnam and *A Star Rises in Hanoi,* a prose collection. These publications tell us that Vietnam was a crucial word for Bang during this period.

A professor of creative writing at Chung-Ang University, Bang worked on the editorial board of *Silcheonmunhak* and is currently the editor-in-chief of *Asia: Magazine of Asian Literature.*

번역 주다희, 안선재

Translated by Dafna Zur and An Son-jae (Brother Anthony of Taizé)

주다희(다프나 주르)는 스탠포드대학교 동아시아 언어문화학과의 조교수로 한국문학, 대중문화, 시각문화, 그리고 아시아의 아동문학을 가르친다. 논문 「'우리는 누구의 전쟁에서 싸우고 있었나?' 남한의 아동소설에서 기억의 구축과 트라우마의 관리」(《아동문학 국제연구》2.2, 2009년 겨울호)와 「남북한 아동문학에 나타난 한국전쟁」(『한국 2010:정치, 경제, 사회』 제4권) 등을 썼고, 『현대한국단편 컬럼비아 앤솔로지』와 《어잴리어』:한국 문학과 문화 저널》, 『밀랍 날개들』 등에 한국문학을 번역하여 수록하였다.

Dafna Zur is an assistant professor at Stanford University, where she teaches courses on Korean literature, popular culture, visual culture, and Asian children's literature in the department of East Asian Languages and Cultures. Her publications include "'Whose War Were We Fighting?' Constructing Memory and Managing Trauma in South Korean Children's Fiction" *International Research in Children's Literature*, 2.2 (December 2009) and "Representations of the Korean War in North and South Korean Children's Literature" *Korea 2010*: Politics, Economy, Society (Vol. 4). Her translations of Korean fiction have appeared in wordwithoutborders.org, *The Columbia Anthology of Modern Korean Short Stories, Azalea: Journal of Korean Literature and Culture*, and *Waxen Wings*.

안선재는 1942년 영국에서 태어나 옥스퍼드대학교에서 중세문학을 공부하다가, 1969년 프랑스 테제 공동체의 수사가 되었다. 1980년부터 한국에서 살고 있다. 서강대학교 교수로 영문학을 가르쳤고 현재는 명예교수이며, 단국대학교 석좌교수이다. 한국문학 30여 권을 영어로 출간했다. 1994년에 한국에 귀화했으며 국가문화훈장 옥관(2008)을 받았다. 현재 아시아왕립학회한국지부 회장이다.

Brother Anthony was born in 1942 in England and completed his studies in the University of Oxford before becoming a member of the Community of Taizé (France) in 1969. Since 1980, he has been living in Korea and teaching at Sogang University, where he is now an Emeritus Professor. Since 2010 he has also been a Chair-Professor at Dankook University. He has published some 30 volumes of English translations of modern Korean literature, including works by Ko Un, So Chong-Ju, Ku Sang, Chon Sang-Pyong etc. For this he was awarded the Korean Government' s Order of Cultural Merit (Jade Crown) in 2008. He took Korean citizenship in 1994 and An Son-jae is his Korean name. Since the start of 2011 he has been President of the Royal Asiatic Society Korea Branch.

감수 **전승희** Edited by Jeon Seung-hee

서울대학교와 하버드대학교에서 영문학과 비교문학으로 박사 학위를 받았으며, 현재 하버드대학교 한국학 연구소의 연구원으로 재직하며 아시아 문예 계간지 《ASIA》 편집위원으로 활동 중이다. 현대 한국문학 및 세계문학을 다룬 논문을 다수 발표했으며, 바흐친의 『장편소설과 민중언어』, 제인 오스틴의 『오만과 편견』 등을 공역했다. 1988년 한국여성연구소의 창립과 《여성과 사회》의 창간에 참여했고, 2002년부터 보스턴 지역 피학대 여성을 위한 단체인 '트랜지션하우스' 운영에 참여해 왔다. 2006년 하버드대학교 한국학 연구소에서 '한국 현대사와 기억'을 주제로 한 워크숍을 주관했다.

Jeon Seung-hee is a member of the Editorial Board of ASIA, is a Fellow at the Korea Institute, Harvard University. She received a Ph.D. in English Literature from Seoul National University and a Ph.D. in Comparative Literature from Harvard University. She has presented and published numerous papers on modern Korean and world literature. She is also a co-translator of Mikhail Bakhtin's *Novel and the People's Culture* and Jane Austen's *Pride and Prejudice*. She is a founding member of the Korean Women's Studies Institute and of the biannual Women's Studies' journal *Women and Society* (1988), and she has been working at 'Transition House', the first and oldest shelter for battered women in New England. She organized a workshop entitled "The Politics of Memory in Modern Korea" at the Korea Institute, Harvard University, in 2006. She also served as an advising committee member for the Asia-Africa Literature Festival in 2007 and for the POSCO Asian Literature Forum in 2008.

바이링궐 에디션 한국 현대 소설 020
새벽 출정

2013년 6월 10일 초판 1쇄 인쇄 | 2013년 6월 15일 초판 1쇄 발행

지은이 방현석 | **옮긴이** 주다희, 안선재 | **펴낸이** 방재석
감수 전승희 | **기획** 정은경, 전성태, 이경재
편집 정수인, 이은혜, 이윤정 | **관리** 박신영 | **디자인** 이춘희

펴낸곳 아시아 | **출판등록** 2006년 1월 31일 제319-2006-4호
주소 서울특별시 동작구 흑석동 100-16
전화 02.821.5055 | **팩스** 02.821.5057 | **홈페이지** www.bookasia.org
ISBN 978-89-94006-73-4 (set) | 978-89-94006-78-9 (04810)
값은 뒤표지에 있습니다.
이 책은 저작권자와 (주)창비의 동의하에 발행합니다.

Bi-lingual Edition Modern Korean Literature 020
Off to Battle at Dawn

Written by Bang Hyeon-seok | **Translated by** Dafna Zur and An Son-jae
Published by Asia Publishers | 100-16 Heukseok-dong, Dongjak-gu, Seoul, Korea
Homepage Address www.bookasia.org | **Tel.** (822).821.5055 | **Fax.** (822).821.5057
First published in Korea by Asia Publishers 2013
ISBN 978-89-94006-73-4 (set) | 978-89-94006-78-9 (04810)